THE RED DRESS

*Sarah Harrison titles available from
Severn House Large Print*

A Dangerous Thing
The Next Room

THE RED DRESS

Sarah Harrison

Severn House Large Print
London & New York

This first large print edition published in Great Britain 2007 by
SEVERN HOUSE LARGE PRINT BOOKS LTD of
9-15 High Street, Sutton, Surrey, SM1 1DF.
First world regular print edition published 2006 by
Severn House Publishers, London and New York.
This first large print edition published in the USA 2007 by
SEVERN HOUSE PUBLISHERS INC., of
595 Madison Avenue, New York, NY 10022.

British Library Cataloguing in Publication Data

Harrison, Sarah, 1946-
  The red dress. - Large print ed.
  1. Evening gowns - Fiction 2. Large type books
  I. Title
  823.9'14[F]

ISBN-13: 978-0-7278-7615-7

Printed and bound in Great Britain by
MPG Books Ltd, Bodmin, Cornwall.

Carolyn

The idea that there should be no secrets between husband and wife was not one to which Carolyn subscribed. On the contrary, she considered that a little secrecy in marriage was no bad thing, provided there was also trust, discretion and respect. Love, of course, was a given.

Carolyn had her secrets – her waxes, her electrolysis, her anti-ageing creams, her herbal remedy habit – and she kept them close. After forty, one had to work harder and spend more in order to look fabulously natural. But there was no need for Oliver to know anything of this. They each had their own bathroom, so she was able to perform her night-time and morning rituals in perfect privacy, joining her husband in bed with a shining face, soft, fragrant skin and silken hair, and slipping away as soon as the alarm went to create her soignée daytime self.

The dress, which she was having made by

her brilliant little woman Mrs Giorgescu, was another of these feminine secrets; Carolyn's biggest. She was going to wear it at their silver wedding party, to knock Oliver's socks off and astonish their friends. For Carolyn was the mistress of the classic, the smart casual, the understated chic. Being tall and slim with fair English skin and hair, that was the style which suited her and that Oliver liked best. She preferred good fabrics – shearling, velvet, silk, suede, soft leather, cashmere – and colours that matched her own – honey, sand, cream, ivory, and tan. Jewellery was real pearls, with discreet gold; and, in the evening, Oliver's diamonds, or on gala occasions her own grandmother's. When Carolyn wore jeans they were YSL, with flat boots and an immaculate white shirt, the collar turned up to create a flattering, light-reflecting frame for her face.

This dress, on the other hand, was to be an exiguous column of crimson satin, perfectly tailored, bias-cut, clinging and flowing round every one of Carolyn's slender curves, revealing more of her flawless pale skin than she had ever before wished or dared to expose.

The night when she would wear it was still several weeks away ... She shivered to think of it.

Her reward for so much careful self-maintenance was the most uxorious husband in Stoke Hetheridge. And – which was even more unusual – one who could dance in both the old-fashioned and more freeform ways, and was prepared to do so the moment the band or disco struck up. Oliver and Carolyn could be relied upon to be first on the floor at hunt balls and village hops alike, putting less able and enterprising husbands in the shade, and turning wallflower wives green with envy.

The Summerbys had money, but no parents extant, and no children. Although it was said that the latter was a secret sadness, the less charitable and more hard-pressed among their friends considered that the three things were not unconnected. Even allowing for Oliver's high octane business acumen and numerous directorships, there was a lot more disposable income if you were not hung about with dependents. But it was generally agreed that the Summerbys were terribly nice and wore their freedom and prosperity lightly. Carolyn especially was a sweetie, guaranteed to throw herself into everything from church restoration to cricket club teas. She also ran Top Notch, a posh hat-hire business, out of the smaller of the Summerbys' two barns (the other had been adapted as a sort of community hall with knobs on, available to all local organisations and individuals for their special events, at knock-down rates).

The ladies of Stoke Hetheridge and environs didn't know how they managed before Carolyn and Top Notch. It was criminal what you had to pay for a serious hat these days, even chic little 'fascinators', comprising an artificial rose and a handful of feathers were well into three figures. At the same time hats, like cars, were emblematic of status, and a person could be judged on what she wore on her head. In the Summerbys' barn, you could equip yourself with anything from a single perfect silk gardenia to a flying saucer of net, straw, grosgrain and ostrich plumes for a fraction of the retail price, and not have it hanging around reproachfully, unworn, in the top of the wardrobe for months afterwards. If you wanted, you could take along an inexpensive titfer purchased in one of the high street chains, or even (considered quite dashing, this) a charity shop, and Carolyn's assistant, clever Saskia, would 'bling it up' for you. All in all a brilliant idea, and one which many of the ladies only wished they'd thought of themselves.

Carolyn knew that it had been a risk employing Saskia. In attracting the cheap-hat brigade, there was always a chance she'd lose the profitable hirers. Fortunately, it didn't work out like that: the cheap-hatters tended to be young, and Saskia spoke their language, so Carolyn succeeded in expanding her market.

Oliver had advised against employing the daughter of Angela and Rob Gorringe, whom they knew socially.

'Never mix business and friendship,' he said. 'If one goes tits up, then so does the other.'

'It'll be fine,' she reassured him. 'She's a lovely girl and so talented.'

'I never said she wasn't. She may well be both of those things, that doesn't make her the right girl to employ here.'

She'd gone ahead and taken Saskia on anyway and within a week she could scarcely imagine life without her. As well as being fresh from a fashion course at St Martins and a whiz with hats, she was fun to have around. Carolyn was pleased to have not only company, but someone who could 'mind the shop' if she was called away. In no time at all they were a team. Even Oliver had to admit grudgingly that the appointment had been a success, though not having seen Saskia for a year or two prior to that he professed himself baffled by her appearance.

'I remember her as being rather a pretty child.'

'Well,' said Carolyn, 'she's no longer a child, for one thing.'

'I can see that.'

'And she's been at art school, remember.'

'What's that got to do with the price of fish?'

'So her style is sort of ... alternative.'

'I'm surprised it hasn't put the customers off.'

'Quite the opposite, it makes them feel current and adventurous.'

'Poor fools.' Oliver chuckled as he took her in his arms. 'I prefer – ' he kissed her – 'this sort of thing.'

Carolyn thought Saskia was like a young Boudicca – tall, square-shouldered, her pale red hair arranged in a mass of small plaits, her ears and nose studded, her forefingers and thumbs be-ringed, a dragon tattooed on her left shoulder. It was only a small dragon, in fact the first time Oliver glimpsed it he had mistaken it for something else.

'Why would a girl from her background want a tattoo at all, let alone a bloody ferret?'

She put him right, adding: 'And background's got nothing to do with it, darling. They all do whatever they want these days. Individualism's the thing.'

'More's the pity.'

'So no comments, please.'

'Comments, moi?'

Carolyn was particularly anxious not to offend Saskia not just because she was fond of her, but because she only had her for a short while. That much had been made plain early on.

'I'm saving to go travelling,' Saskia had announced in her deep, husky voice.

'Anywhere in particular?' Carolyn had asked.

'Cuba, Latin America ... I want to soak up a few influences.'

'And then you'll come back and blow us all away with your designs.'

'That's the idea,' said Saskia.

In any event, Saskia was a tremendous asset to Top Notch, and her unusual appearance flattered the customers by making them feel they were free spirits, capable of being that little bit outrageous. Carolyn also observed that her youth and strangeness set up a sort of collective hormonal jangle in the females of Stoke Hetheridge. They almost flirted with her.

'Oh, Saskia,' they cried. 'Do you think I could? Do you honestly think I could carry it off? What the hell, let's live dangerously for once!'

Carolyn's friend Angela Gorringe, Saskia's mama, confessed herself pleasantly surprised by her daughter's popularity.

'It's quite extraordinary,' she confided to Carolyn at the church tower wine-tasting. 'At home we see no evidence whatever of interpersonal skills, but it appears she can pull them out of the hat – ' here she barked with laughter at her own joke – 'when required!'

'She certainly can,' said Carolyn. 'Everyone adores her, and it's astonishing what she can do with a five-pound straw from BHS. I only wish we could keep her, she'll be awfully hard to replace.'

Angela laid an imploring hand on Carolyn's arm. 'Pay her less, for God's sake ... We so don't want her to go.'

'Why not?'

'Saskia? Off on her own? To South America? How long have you got? She has no plan, no itinerary, she's totally disorganized, she's hopelessly trusting.'

'Yes,' agreed Carolyn, 'that could be a problem. But still, Angela, she has to follow her dream.'

'Forgive me for saying so,' said Angela, 'but there speaks the child-free woman.'

Carolyn did forgive her. At one time it would not have been so easy, but these days, with six godchildren and as many nephews and nieces, she had come to appreciate the advantages of being an affectionate, disinterested adult. A young person, especially a young woman, often needed an older confidante with whom there was no agenda, none of the baggage of the parent–child relationship. Not that Carolyn would ever have abused her position – the idea of courting popularity or undermining that relationship was abhorrent. On the contrary, she saw herself as a combination of sounding board and lightning conductor, a useful resource to be made use of by both parties. She imagined that her status in these young people's lives must be something akin to being a young grandparent, a role which though denied to her she understood to be warmly enjoyable and rewarding.

Oliver had a few godchildren himself but regarded his involvement as wholly secular and financial, restricted to generous cheques on birthdays and at Christmas, and attendance at rites of passage. He made no bones about the fact that he was completely unqualified to give spiritual guidance, let alone to act in loco parentis, and that parents selected him at their own risk, for his money alone. He accepted his wife's more hands-on approach in a spirit of affectionate indulgence.

The Summerbys had never discussed their own childlessness; it was not an issue. They had expected children would come along, but as the years went by and nothing happened they had not been so disappointed that they'd wanted to put themselves through the depressing business of fertility tests, and IVF. Adoption had never even been mentioned. Oliver was not one of those men who needed the ego-boost of a son and heir, and Carolyn found an outlet for her maternal instincts elsewhere.

When Carolyn told Oliver about Angela Gorringe's worries, he said: 'A case requiring your delicate mediation, I think.'

Carolyn had laughed and said it was none of her business, but at the same time she could see that there might be something she could do, even if it was only encouraging Saskia to be a little more organized and so allay her mother's fears.

It was the end of March and the beginning of spring; a time of daffodils and frost, icy nights and lengthening days. A season when Carolyn especially loved the warm, elegant

14

spaces of the Top Notch barn, the round fireplace filled with smooth stones over which flames licked and rippled like water, the hidden speakers which wafted Katie Melua, Miles Davis and Ella Fitzgerald into every corner at the flick of a switch, the clever lighting which adjusted itself to the natural light ... And, of course, the hats, blooming like blossom on their treelike stands, scattered over the long table like presents, hanging like trophies on the walls ... Each one repaying its investment three, four times over in the first six months. It would not have been true to say Carolyn didn't care about profit. She may not in the strictest sense have needed the money, but its value in terms of her independence and self-esteem was incalculable. Still, her greatest pleasure came in marrying the right hat with the right person. She had a good eye and was never less than honest about whether a hat suited the wearer. She was also a great believer in having the clothes first, then the shoes, and the hat last: you had to be comfortable to look good (her own mother had always maintained that an older woman wore her shoes on her face), and there was no point in having the hat of one's dreams if one then had to go out and spend a small fortune on something to go with it. Also, this meant that a putative hirer could bring along whatever it was they intended to wear and try on the toute ensemble right there – she'd had two changing cubicles put in for the purpose. There was also a shelf of plain court shoes in standard sizes and different colours, with varying heel heights: some hats required that you walk tall.

Carolyn loved the moment when she unlocked the barn in the morning and could savour her success. There was always a faint smell of vanilla – a fan of pods hung over the fire – and fresh coffee, which she made every day. After all, she knew most of her customers personally; when she'd first started the hat thing they'd come to the house and the exchange would be as much social as it was commercial. She wanted to preserve that informal, welcoming, woman-to-woman feeling, so coffee, tea and mineral water were always on offer – wine, too, on her spring and autumn open days – and there were tiny, single-mouthful Florentines from the patisserie in the market. In the corner between the fire and the window were two sofas and a low table so people could confer, or just wait, in comfort. Fresh flowers were delivered every Thursday. The barn was her kingdom.

This morning Carolyn let herself in as usual at nine thirty, an hour before Saskia was due to arrive and an hour and a half before opening time. Experience had shown that there were few takers before eleven, but that people liked to come at lunchtime, and then again in the late afternoon and early evening, so although Saskia left at five, she would stay here until six thirty, or whenever the last client left. She would not have dreamed, no matter how picky or indecisive someone was, of showing them the door.

Saskia's corner was analogous to the 'messy play' area in an infants school, with a large table strewn with pots of pencils, fabric, ribbon, binding, feathers and artificial flowers, a fiercely practical workbox, and an old seaman's chest (Carolyn had found it in a junk shop) full of more materials, and a bookcase with magazines, files, folders and sketchbooks. Carolyn approved of this island of creative chaos. In her otherwise immaculately ordered room it struck an authentically artistic note, and she liked the sense it provided of an atelier – the work going on in full view, the process made open.

She flicked several switches – fire, lights, music – and went into the microscopic galley kitchen to put the kettle on. The

17

Norah Jones CD she had been playing the evening before breathed softly around her. The thick whisper of the kettle heating blended with the backing track. Oliver had gone to Dubai for a few days, she felt a little melancholy at the thought of the cooling, empty house to which she would return later. After nearly twenty-five years of marriage she still missed him when he went away. A quarter of a century, it was incredible! Maybe if they'd had children they would feel older, more careworn, more responsible, but because they didn't, the two of them seemed – to Carolyn at least – to have scarcely changed since they met. Which had been at another wedding, the union of two Turkish Cypriots at the Connaught Rooms. Oliver was the bride's boss, Carolyn her flatmate: they were both a little out of place and had encountered one another in the act of pinning ten-pound notes to the bride's dress. Oliver had made some whispered reference to the effect that both bride and frock were of a size to ensure a down payment on a very decent semi, Carolyn had laughed, and one thing had led to another. Both agreed that they were absolutely not each other's type – Oliver had always preferred buxom brunettes and Carolyn favoured slim, sensitive, Nigel

18

Havers types. Instead of which ... they had gazed at one another, puzzled and enchanted: Carolyn the slender blonde; Oliver the curly-headed goliath.

They had been together ever since, defying the predictions and outlasting a good many of their friends. 'Still crazy after all these years' might have been their theme song. Carolyn's mental picture of the two of them was of a great black ship (Oliver), reminiscent of Masefield's 'dirty British coaster', clipping through mountainous seas, with a kite on a string (herself) attached to its 'salt-caked smoke stack', bobbing and fluttering high in the air; free, but secure.

This early morning hour was not for work, but for recalibration; it was a period of tranquil adjustment, so that when others, starting with Saskia, began to arrive the barn would be warm, fragrant and welcoming – an oasis of peace and colour in people's busy, pressured lives. She poured herself a herbal tea, checked the diary for returns and collections, glanced over the accounts, and inspected the stock, trying on the occasional hat herself to make sure that her eye hadn't deserted her. Not every one suited her, of course, she had to have hats for every age, complexion and shape, but

19

she needed to be able to speak with friendly authority about the different styles and for that it was necessary for her to keep in touch with what was here.

At ten thirty there was the unmistakable sound of the ancient deux-chevaux coming down the drive, and being parked round the corner, between the side of the barn and the house. From politeness, Carolyn referred to this area as staff parking, but actually it was to keep the DCV out of the way. There was nothing the matter with the car's outward appearance, it was amusing and character-ful, a classic young person's banger; but if, as they said, a woman's car was an extension of her handbag, then she hoped never to glimpse what lurked inside Saskia's capacious tribal-weave tote.

Now she greeted Carolyn in her discon-certingly chocolatey voice: 'Hi, how's it going?'

'Well, thanks.' Carolyn recognized the greeting as formulaic but couldn't help replying as if it wasn't. 'Coffee?'

'Oh God, yeah!' Saskia dumped her bag on the end of the work table. 'It's absolutely perishing out there.'

'Lovely, though.'

'Caffeine will make it look a whole lot lovelier.'

'There you are.' Carolyn handed Saskia the Blonde at Heart mug and watched as she took her first reviving sips.

This morning Saskia wore her usual jeans and Hiawatha boots, with an assortment of amusingly layered tops, all anyhow, with one black bra strap boldly and carelessly revealed. Carolyn, coming from a generation to whom a visible bra strap was on a par with undone flies, was getting used to this robust attitude to underpinnings and on the whole rather approved of it. Bra straps, thongs, the unashamed flaunting of pregnancies – all showed the enviably healthy body-confidence of the young.

'That's better,' said Saskia. 'Do you mind if I eat something? I was running late and didn't have any breakfast.'

'There's nothing much over here, but you can pop over and make toast.'

'It's okay, I got something at the garage.' She returned to the bag, put down her mug and fished out a cereal bar. 'Only one per cent fat,' she said as she pulled down the wrapper. 'As recommended by that food-Nazi on the telly.'

'What about sugar?' asked Carolyn. 'There has to be something to make it palatable.'

'Who said anything about palatable?'

Saskia made a face as she chewed. 'Mm, yum, cage sweepings, bird food and lycra.'

'It looks absolutely horrible.'

'That's why it's good for you,' said Saskia. 'You chuck it away after one mouthful. But it hasn't worked this time, I'm starving.'

She finished the bar, threw the wrapper in the basket under the table, dusted her hands together and picked up her coffee.

'Right, I'm ready. Bring it on.'

Top Notch didn't close at lunchtime, and the barn was so nice that very often they didn't go anywhere. Carolyn prohibited the eating of sandwiches in the barn itself – the smell of tuna or chicken tikka hung around unacceptably – so Saskia sometimes took off for half an hour, or ate outside, sitting in the driver's seat of the DCV with her head-phones on. Carolyn herself either didn't bother at all, or popped back to the house. She could see the barn from the side window in the kitchen, and in the unlikely event that a client had to press the buzzer it sounded in the house as well.

They were quiet today and she suggested Saskia join her for lunch.

'I've got some smoked salmon and blinis, how does that sound?'

'Lovely ... What are blinis?'

'Pancakes – like scotch pancakes, have you ever had those?'

'I don't think so, anyway they sound great, I'll eat anything, thanks.'

Carolyn locked the barn and they walked down the drive and over the wooden hump-backed bridge, beneath which moorhens and mallards sculled about in the green waters of the moat.

'I still think this is all so incredible,' said Saskia. 'It must feed your soul, living in a place like this.'

'We're very lucky,' agreed Carolyn. 'I never take it for granted.'

'Where did you live before you came here?'

'We were in London for a while. In Holland Park.'

'I bet that was gorgeous too.'

'Well – ' Carolyn opened the front door – 'it was different, of course. A town house, but it had its own character. And it was our first home together, so I was sad to leave it.'

Saskia gazed wonderingly at the ancient beams, the linenfold panelling, the golden wood floors. 'Wow, Carolyn ... it's all so amazing.'

'Come on through – does it feel cold? I can press override.'

'I'm fine.'

'There's an aga in here, anyway.'

'Of course there is.'

They went into the kitchen, and Carolyn pulled a chair back from the table.

'Sit down.'

'Can I do anything?'

'There's nothing to do. I'm going to get a couple of things out of the fridge and throw the blinis in the microwave for a few seconds. Would you like a glass of wine?'

'No thanks.'

Carolyn opened the fridge. 'Beer? There's Budweisers in here.'

Saskia hesitated. 'Would that be okay?'

'Of course!' Carolyn got out a bottle and flipped the top on the opener at the side of the fridge. 'I don't drink it, and Oliver's away.' She put the bottle on the table. 'Glasses are in the cupboard.'

'Bottle's fine.'

Carolyn poured mineral water for herself, put cream cheese and smoked salmon on the table and the blinis on a plate in the microwave.

'This is nice,' she said. 'Thanks for keeping me company.'

'Where's he gone?' Carolyn sensed that Saskia wasn't quite sure how to refer to Oliver – Mr was too formal and old-fashioned, his Christian name too familiar, your husband somehow inappropriate.

'He's in Dubai.'

'Rather him than me,' was Saskia's response.

Carolyn put the blinis on the table. 'Tuck in. However you like.' Out of politeness, she kicked off herself, spreading cream cheese and folding smoked salmon on top. 'Mm – I love this, it's such a good mixture.'

Saskia copied. 'For dying,' she agreed, munching and pointing to her bulging cheek. 'I'm going to tell Mum to get some of these.'

Carolyn remembered that twenty, tattoo and plaits notwithstanding, was not very old these days. Girls of twenty lived at home and had their washing and cooking done for them. At twenty she herself had been receptionist in the Fyfield Gallery in Mayfair, but Saskia wouldn't think twice about placing an order for blinis with her mother.

'Have you been to Dubai, Saskia?' she asked.

'No, and it so doesn't appeal to me. All that stinking rich artificiality, all those fat cats—' She stopped as she realized what she'd said. 'Sorry, I didn't mean – you know.'

Carolyn laughed. 'That's all right, it's not Oliver's favourite place either. I think he'd say pretty much the same thing.'

'Do you ever go with him? When he goes somewhere nice? If he goes somewhere nice...'

'Hardly ever. I did go once to Hong Kong, but on the whole ... His time there is one long meeting. And anyway, there's my business – I can't go swanning off at a moment's notice even if I wanted to. I'd rather wait and go away together when we're neither of us working.'

'Makes sense. May I?'

'Help yourself.' Carolyn pushed the plate over. 'Tuck in.'

'Only they're so delish...'

Watching Saskia eat, Carolyn reflected that whatever Oliver might say, youth needed no gilding. The strength, freshness and vitality of sweet and twenty was an absolute – it could not be bought, or improved upon. It was itself. At forty-five one could be slim, but the flesh tone was never so firm, nor the skin so smooth, as it had been two decades before. Hair could be nourished, styled and enhanced, make-up carefully applied to look like no make-up, clothes carefully chosen and nails manicured, but what was gone was gone for ever. Saskia, munching voraciously on her blinis and salmon, was perfect, just as she was.

She affected the style which Oliver claimed not to like for no other reason than that she could.

Now she finished, with a sigh of satisfaction, and stifled a burp.

'Really, really nice. Cheers, Carolyn.'

'Pleasure. Coffee?'

'Go on then.'

Pouring hot water into the cafetière, Carolyn asked casually: 'So how are the travel plans going?'

'I'm about halfway there. In terms of money, I mean. With a bit of luck I'll be able to take off in September – perhaps I shouldn't say that, would that be okay with you?'

'Absolutely – it's useful to have some idea when I'll be losing you, because I hope you know you'll be very hard to replace.'

'Maybe,' said Saskia, 'you'll find someone with a better car.'

Carolyn began to say there was nothing the matter with Saskia's car, but realized she was being teased.

'It's more secure parked out of the way.'

'Yeah, right.'

Carolyn poured coffee and opened a packet of fudge, which she put in front of Saskia. 'Do have a bit, or I shall be tempted.'

'I don't know why you worry, you're like

an absolute rail.'

'That's because I avoid fudge.'

'In that case, happy to help you out...' Saskia helped herself. 'You should hear what my mum says about you.'

'Nobody wants to hear what other people say.'

'No seriously, she thinks you're the dog's bollocks.'

'That's very sweet of her.'

'Sweet?' It was just as well Saskia had finished the fudge or she would have choked on it. 'Mum doesn't do sweet.'

'Then I'll accept the compliment grace-fully,' said Carolyn. She let a moment pass, and then added: 'I bet she worries about you.'

'Is that what she said?'

Saskia's eyes had narrowed; a white lie was definitely called for.

'No, she hasn't mentioned it. I just know how I'd feel if it was my daughter.'

'Everyone goes travelling. I didn't have a gap year, so this is it.'

'Tell me,' said Carolyn, 'what's the itiner-ary?'

'Heathrow to Lima.'

'And then?'

'Whatever seems like a good idea.'

★ ★ ★

Oliver rang at eight o'clock that evening – seven his time, as he was about to leave for a business dinner.

'I fully expect it to be insufferably dull,' he said. 'Would that you were here, my darling.'

'Sounds as if I'm well out of it. You should hear Saskia's views on Dubai.'

'She's been?'

'Of course not, she's twenty, she has views on everything.'

'I expect she's right, too. Did you do your wise-woman thing about Argentina or wherever it is?'

'I put a toe in the water.'

'And got it bitten off?'

'No, but she doesn't need advice, from anyone. She's a free spirit.'

'Good, well, speaking of free spirits, I hear the call of the desert-dry martini.'

'Off you go, have fun.'

'As if. Night, darling.'

'Night.'

Carolyn poured herself a glass of Alsace Riesling, and turned on Classic FM as she made scrambled egg to go with the remains of the smoked salmon. Sipping and stirring, she dreamed of the red dress.

On Friday, the day Oliver was due back, Carolyn left Saskia in charge of Top Notch and went for a fitting with Mrs Giorgescu in the local university town. Carolyn no longer wanted the hassle of London, unless it was for a night out.

Mrs Giorgescu lived on her own, and Mr Giorgescu was never mentioned. Her flat was in an area known as the Mile; the part of town whose only connection with gown was that about half the student population were housed in its maze of Victorian working men's terraced cottages. Mrs Giorgescu complained about the students – their noise, their mess, their magnetic attraction for thieves – but Carolyn sensed the affection beneath the complaints.

The flat was neat – what could be seen of it, Carolyn was always ushered straight into the sewing room, and the other doors were kept discreetly closed. Even the lavatory, on those occasions when Carolyn had needed to use it, was devoid of those accessories, pictures, humorous texts and bog-side books that could provide a clue to the owner's taste.

Mrs Giorgescu had made things for Carolyn before, and her measurements had not changed: the swathe of red satin was cut and tacked in place on the size 10 dummy, the offcuts neatly folded on the work table by the window.

'Now,' said Mrs Giorgescu, 'you take your clothes off, please, and we give it a go.'

To begin with Carolyn had felt a little shy stripping down to her underwear in front of the dressmaker, but now it held no more embarrassment than undressing for the doctor.

'You wear bra?' asked Mrs Giorgescu.

'I've got the right one on, don't worry.'

'Good girl.'

Standing there while the beginnings of the red dress were eased off the dummy, Carolyn was glad of the gas fire.

'Cold, hmm?' Mrs Giorgescu nodded and pursed her lips. 'Not surprising – thin, thin, thin.'

'This is my natural weight.'

'We see,' said Mrs Giorgescu, dropping the skirt of the dress over Carolyn's head, and easing it down. She smelt of aniseed and her palms were calloused – where they touched, the dry skin whispered against the satin. But they were also gentle, careful hands, capable of the most delicate and intricate work. And safe hands, too – Carolyn knew the dress would be flawless.

Mrs Giorgescu tilted the mirror so that it framed the whole of Carolyn, top to toe. She placed her hands on Carolyn's hips and narrowed her eyes like a marksman taking aim.

'Hmm ... we get there, you see what you think...'

The next half an hour was pure peace, as the dressmaker pinned, stitched, stood, bent and knelt to make her adjustments. There was no sound in the room but her breathing, and that of the gas fire, and her occasional small grunts and exclamations as she worked. Carolyn relaxed into what was a kind of sensory flotation tank, in which she was relieved of the burden of identity, and activity, and purpose and decision-making – there was nothing to do but be there and be still, a body to be worked on.

When Mrs Giorgescu was done, she undid the pins at the side of the dress and helped Carolyn step out. She held up two fingers.

'Twice more, only. We be done.'

'Wonderful. I can't wait – you're so clever.'

'Oh! Ts-ts-ts – never mind!' Mrs Giorgescu went into a positive paroxysm of brusque self-deprecation, and laid the dress carefully on the work table. Then she watched as Carolyn put her clothes back on. It was evident she was going to unburden herself of a comment, Carolyn could sense her whirring and humming, winding up to it like a clock about to strike.

'How long you been married?' she asked.

'The party – how long for?'

'Twenty-five years.'

'God Almighty, that is a long time these days!'

'I suppose it is. We're very lucky.'

'Your husband loves you.'

'He does.' Carolyn took a small hairbrush out of her handbag and tidied her hair in the mirror.

'He likes you to be so thin?'

Carolyn replaced the brush and snapped the bag shut. 'He must do. I'm the same weight today as I was the day we met.'

Suddenly Mrs Giorgescu stepped forward and boldly, even fiercely, grasped Carolyn's right breast in one hand, and her left buttock in the other, giving both an impatient shake. 'Is nothing there!'

Carolyn stepped away, laughing to cover her shock.

'I can't help it.'

'Never mind, never mind...' Mrs Giorgescu flung both hands in the air and chuckled. 'You make good model!'

On the way home, once she'd got over her mild indignation, Carolyn wondered if she had indeed got thinner. She had certainly not tried to lose weight – it wasn't a problem for her – but maybe the pounds had been slipping away without her noticing. Out on the open road she pulled into a lay-by and flipped down the driver's mirror to examine her face. Perhaps there were a few more fine wrinkles around the eyes ... a hint of incipient seaming on the upper lip ... No need for a chip-and-chocolate-fest, but she must make an effort to drink plenty of water and plump up the fat cells. Turning her head this way and that, she ran a hand down her neck. The last thing she wanted was to look scrawny in the red dress.

As she turned into the drive, she saw Oliver's black Porsche Cayenne parked at a careless angle outside the garage, and her heart leapt. He must have caught an earlier flight – he was back!

She pulled up alongside the barn and got out to tell Saskia that she would take an extra few minutes. Before she as much as opened the door she heard voices, and assumed they had a customer, but when she went in, Oliver was there, standing in the middle of the floor in a Grecian nymph attitude, one hand raised, the other flying behind him. On his head was Top Notch's most extravagant creation, a riot of violet tulle and velvet with a purple maribout plume. Saskia was sitting on her work table, laughing uncontrollably.

'Oliver...?' Carolyn began to laugh too, it was infectious, and he did look ridiculous. 'What's this, an audition for Charlie's Aunt?'

'Darling!'

He whipped off the hat and shied it like a frisbee to Saskia who – thank heavens! – caught it. 'See what happens when your back's turned?'

'It's so lovely that you're home.'

'It's lovely to be home.' He kissed her on the lips. Saskia got off the table and replaced the hat on its stand. Her back was discreetly towards them. For the first time Carolyn noticed the voluptuous curve of her waist, the flare of her bottom, and the smooth ridge of exposed flesh above the waistband of her jeans – which in fact was scarcely a waistband at all since it sagged low enough to reveal a shadow of rear cleavage – that cleft which was so embarrassing and repellent in a male labourer was, Carolyn suspected, sweetly alluring in a young woman.

'Where've you been, anyway?' asked Oliver.

'Oh, I had to see a client who couldn't get over here.' Carolyn shot Saskia a warning glance, but she was affecting extreme busyness and wouldn't catch her eye.

'I should make it clear,' Oliver went on, 'that Saskia was running a tight ship till I came in. The responsibility for mucking about was entirely mine.'

'I don't doubt it for a moment.'

'I apologize for being a bad influence.'

Saskia still didn't look up from her work, but she did smile.

'Anyway,' said Carolyn, 'now the boss is back, the fun's over. Off you go, I'll see you in – ' she checked her watch – 'a couple of hours, customers permitting.'

'Hear that?' Oliver addressed Saskia. 'I put a girdle round the earth and she says she'll see me in a couple of hours. She's a hard woman.'

Saskia laughed, her eyes still on her work. Carolyn opened the door.

'On your way.'

'I'm gone.'

He kissed her as he left and whispered: 'Can't wait...'

Carolyn closed the door behind him and went into the kitchen to make tea. The clarinet concerto which had been drowned by their talk, now wafted in the air like thought bubbles.

Oliver was especially amorous that evening

and took her upstairs the moment she got in. Afterwards he fell back with a huge sigh, rubbing his belly with both hands like a man who'd feasted well.

'Too good, my darling ... There's nothing like deferred gratification to sharpen the appetite.'

He put out an arm and scooped her to his side. 'I adore you, you know.'

'And I you,' she said.

He pulled his head back to look at her. 'You don't have to say that.'

'I know.'

'Only you sounded – never mind.'

'Sounded what?'

'On autopilot.'

'I'm sorry, I can't think why.'

'Is it because I was distracting the staff from their duties.'

'Yes.'

'You sin-binned me for that.' He pulled his head back again. 'Surely I'm forgiven now?'

'You are,' she said, kissing him.

'Good.' He settled back, squeezing her shoulders so that she could feel his heart-beat against her face. 'I should think so.'

Oliver had an enormous capacity for happiness. It was one of the most attractive things about him, his ability to take pleasure in the good things of life; of which in his case there were plenty. But still, many rich, successful men were ground down by care, travel, jet-lag, school fees, ever more demanding wives and the heel-biting of ambitious younger colleagues. Oliver's face was broad and smooth, his eyes bright, his laugh always ready to ring out – and this fortunate disposition was infectious. Carolyn knew herself to be potentially neurotic, even depressive, but marriage to Oliver had stabilized her. If she had sounded 'on autopilot' in responding to his (frequently expressed) adoration it was not through lack of feeling – far from it – but because of a twitch of that latent neurosis.

Which, she told herself as she showered, was nonsense, and probably due to Mrs Giorgescu's tactlessness. Carolyn spread the creamy lather over her neat breasts, her concave belly and sleek arms and legs. Not bad for forty-five ... There was nothing to worry about.

Over the next fortnight, apart from odd day trips to Frankfurt, Brussels and Dublin, Oliver was in the UK. The full hi-honey-I'm-home Monty as he called it, though in fact he actually worked right there for some of the time, in his large sunlit office above the garage, in the smaller of the two barns.

Life when Oliver was around had a different tempo and texture for Carolyn. Knowing that he was nearby, she became more relaxed and laissez faire. When things were quiet at Top Notch she went back and forth to the house more often, and even occasionally pottered in the garden while keeping an eye out for customers. From one side of the garden she could see Oliver sitting at his desk at the computer, reading, or on the phone. When he talked on the phone he usually stared out of the window, but though he seemed to be looking at her his mind's eye was usually focused on who-ever he was talking to, and he rarely registered her presence.

One such day Carolyn was in the garden when Maude Hillyard's Audi estate came down the drive. She immediately headed back towards the barn. Framed by the window, Oliver was talking on his phone, his free arm wrapped over his head as if cutting out excess noise. When Carolyn reached the barn, at about the same time as Maude's car pulled up, she was surprised to see Saskia sitting in the front seat of the DCV, mobile glued to her ear. Catching Carolyn's politely enquiring eye she waggled a hand and grimaced an apology while saying – Carolyn could read her lips – 'Got to go.'

Carolyn turned to greet Maude and almost subliminally saw the flash of white shirt sleeve, like a flag, as twenty yards away in his office Oliver, too, put the phone down.

'Sorry!' said Saskia, hurrying in. 'Had to make a call – only been there a moment, I promise.'

Maude smiled indulgently as they followed her. 'Oh to be young...'

That evening as she made salad dressing, Carolyn gazed at the tiny globules of balsamic vinegar suspended in the thick, green olive oil. They'd remain like that, unamalgamated, intact, until she shook the jar vigorously when they'd burst and break up, pervading the oil and turning the mixture cloudy, with an edge of sourness.

Oliver's next trip of any length was to the States. His flight was on the Saturday, but he left the day before to take in a meeting in London. Carolyn had a dress fitting on the Friday, and emailed the client list to say she would be closing at five. Saskia had offered to stay and hold the fort, but Carolyn guessed she would have other fish to fry on a Friday night, and told her to go home.

Mrs Giorgescu had worked her magic. The dress was now unmistakably a dress, with only last-minute adjustments left to make. These included the long zip up the back, which lay on the work table like an exotic dead snake with its mouth open.

Carolyn held up her arms, and Mrs Giorgescu slipped the dress over her head. There was something ritualistic in the movement, as if Carolyn were a postulant, or being prepared for sacrifice. The satin slithered down her arms, over her face, neck and shoulders, down over her body to the floor ... incredibly soft and smooth and only slightly cooler than blood temperature ... like being swathed in cream.

But when Carolyn looked in the mirror she felt a plunge of the bitterest disappointment. Something was wrong! Not with the dress itself, but with the reflection of herself wearing it. For so long she had carried a mental picture of herself in the dress – her skin luminously white, her slenderness made voluptuous by the sheen of the material, her pale hair reflecting its vibrant colour ... Instead, she saw a thin, anxious-looking, middle-aged woman, with small frown-lines like inverted commas between her brows, and a suggestion of ribbiness above the dress's sleek décolleté. Her arms were

41

toned, but the skin on the underside was a little crepey, and the roots of her hair, exposed to the strong sunlight in Mrs Giorgescu's atelier, were not ash blonde at all, but a dull grey.

Mrs Giorgescu was looking over her shoulder. In the mirror, their eyes met.

'The dress is good?'

'It's very good, Mrs Giorgescu. You are clever.'

'You don't like.' This was said without hostility, in a shrewd, matter-of-fact voice that brooked no argument. Carolyn was mortified.

'I do! I do – I love it!'

Mrs Giorgescu shook her head. She took the sides of the dress and pinched them between her blunt fingers.

'For sure is too big.'

'No it's not. Of course it isn't. Once it has the zip—'

'You lost weight some more. I must take in.'

'I'm quite sure I haven't,' insisted Carolyn, against the evidence of that incriminating inch of material, which Mrs Giorgescu, having made her point, now released with a slight flourish.

'I'm not looking my best,' Carolyn conceded. 'I'm rather tired.'

'Rest, sleep. Eat! You want I take it in?'

'No, don't. I shall plump up, I promise.'

'Not long now.'

'No, that's true.'

'Brides, they always get thin and more thin,' said Mrs Giorgescu. 'They so excited, even the fat ones burn up.'

'Maybe that's what it is, then,' said Carolyn hopefully. 'I'm over-excited.'

Mrs Giorgescu gave her a tap on the bottom. 'But you not a bride, but grown-up.'

That was a polite way of putting it – sort of, thought Carolyn, as she leaned forward for the dressmaker to ease the satin over her shoulders. She was glad to be putting on her safer, more concealing clothes as the dress was returned to its hanger. Mrs Giorgescu swathed it in its plastic bag and turned to face her with a combative air.

'So – I put in zip and leave dress as is.'

'Yes please. It's perfect, really.'

'When you collect?'

'The week after next – shall we say Friday?'

'Day before your party?'

'That's right. You do have a good memory.'

Mrs Giorgescu came with her to the door. 'You have shawl?'

'Not with me, no.'

43

'I mean for party.'

'I do have pashminas ... But not one that matches, and besides it'll be June, I'm hoping—'

Another bossy tap, this time on the arm. 'Wear shawl. To begin anyway. Less skin.'

This time Carolyn got only a couple of hundred yards before pulling into a side street and bursting into tears. When she got home, she poured herself first a glass of Shiraz and then a deep, scented bath. She tuned the radio to Classic FM, lit candles though it wasn't dark, and undressed out of sight of any mirrors. Then she lowered herself into the perfumed bubbles and lay there for the best part of an hour, as though the bath were amniotic fluid and she waiting to be reborn.

As she was getting dry she heard the phone ring in the bedroom. Once she was in her thick, soft chenille dressing gown, the hood over her wet hair, she pressed play to hear the message, but none had been left. Dialling, she found the number of Oliver's mobile recorded. He'd rung! For the first time that evening she looked at herself in the glass. She was pink and warm from the bath, her hair slightly curly because it was wet. Her eyes were bright, her skin fresh and clear. She looked neither old nor scrawny. She glanced at the time – seven forty-five – and then pressed the return call button. His voicemail answered, but instead of leaving a message she went downstairs and found the number of the hotel.

'May I speak to Mr Summerby, please? He's with you for one night. This is his wife.'

'One moment please, Mrs Summerby...' There was a pause and a brief burst of Brandenburg. 'He's not answering in his room.'

'In the bar perhaps? He just rang, and I'm returning his call.'

'Hold on please Mrs Summerby, we'll see if we can find him for you.'

There followed more Brandenburg, during which Carolyn wondered why on earth she had felt the need to justify herself. She pictured the phone being borne ceremonially into first the bar, then the hotel dining room ... Or would they simply bring Oliver to the telephone? Now that the mobile was king this would be a fairly unusual circumstance.

'Mrs Summerby?'

'Yes, hallo.'

'I'm afraid we don't seem to be able to locate Mr Summerby at this moment in time. His key's not here, but perhaps he went out and took it with him.'

'Oh, right ... never mind. Thank you for trying.'

She rang off and then dialled the mobile again. Oliver's voicemail message had that studied informality which had travelled over the Atlantic in recent years: 'Hi, this is Oliver, sorry I'm tied up...'

When it had finished, she said: 'Darling, it's me, at about – eight fifteen? So sorry I missed you earlier, and now you're out on the town. If you get a chance to call before the flight, please do. I know how busy you'll be after that, so hope it all goes well. All my love, miss you. Bye.'

When she'd rung off, the house felt oppressively still. Before her the weekend, normally so inviting, yawned drearily. Not that she hadn't got plenty to do, there were jobs she always kept for when Oliver was away, she would work in the garden, and friends had asked her to supper tomorrow evening, but none of it filled her with enthusiasm. Perhaps in the morning things would look different.

But when after a fitful night she woke up earlier than usual it was raining – no soft summer drizzle but a solid downpour that entirely precluded gardening, and made it so unseasonably dark that she had to have the light on while she drank her morning coffee.

At half past eight the phone rang. It was Oliver, calling her from the departure lounge.

'Sorry I missed you last night.'

'I called back, but you must have gone out just after.'

'Anyway, I'm sure we'll speak over the next couple of days.'

'Don't worry,' she said. 'I know what it's like. But I do miss you.'

'Darling...' he murmured appreciatively. 'Have a nice weekend.'

'It's pouring here.'

'Is it? I'm in airport world. But what's that thing they say about rain early on?'

'Rain before seven, fine before eleven.'

'That's it. You'll be out there hedging and ditching by lunchtime.'

'I hope so.'

There was a tiny, awkward pause, which Oliver ended by saying briskly, 'Okay, we're boarding. Bye, darling.'

'Bye...'

Wise old saws notwithstanding, the rain hammered down all morning, and eased off only slightly in the afternoon, going from flat-out to cruise mode and settling in for the duration. She wished she had been more cheerful, more 'up' with Oliver on the

47

phone. She had wanted more than anything to speak to him and when finally given the opportunity she had been dull and plaintive, which was unlike her. She vowed that when – if – he called from New York she would be her old self, the lively, loving Carolyn that he longed to come back to.

Gardening was out, and the house was, as ever, immaculate. The Summerbys had no pets nor ever wanted any, but at this moment Carolyn almost wished she had a dog that in return for a little attention, food and a walk, would give her its unconditional affection and companionship. Or maybe she should acquire a trophy cat, an elegant oriental with long legs, almond eyes and a kink in its tail, who would become her familiar ... The white witch of Hetheridge Hall. She was lonely.

In an attempt to shake off this un-characteristic self-pity she went over to the barn. The window of Oliver's office was blank and dark as she hurried by beneath her umbrella.

Once inside Top Notch her mood im-proved slightly. This was her place, the tran-quil domain over which she had complete control. Because Oliver was not usually here, it was possible to miss him less. She decided to pretend that this was a normal

48

working day, turning on the lights and the music, lighting some of the vanilla candles, and putting on the kettle for coffee. The shifting population of hats were like friends. Or perhaps pets, with their fur and flowers and feathers, so beautiful and tactile, her conduit to the outside world.

Carolyn set herself to work, stocktaking, and bringing the diary and the books up to date. Ella Fitzgerald sang of saying goodbye, and then of turning Manhattan into an isle of joy. She thought of Oliver, up there where the air was rarefied, airborne over the Atlantic ... Gradually she recalibrated, and her self-esteem returned. She realized that fond though she was of Saskia, it was pleasant to be here without her. After all she had started this business, and run it for years, on her own, and would do so again. Saskia was a nice girl, and talented, but by no means indispensable. Carolyn decided that far from trying to dissuade her from going to South America, she would wish her Godspeed and send her on her way with a wave and a smile.

Trying this idea on for size, she went over to Saskia's work table and pushed it back a little, making more space. Then she sat down on it and surveyed the barn from this angle. Her eye fell on the hat that Oliver had been fooling around with that day when he got back early, now hanging at a rakish angle on its stand. She smiled at the mental picture of his face beneath it, but only for a second, because something disturbing in the memory nudged her with its cold snout and made her shiver.

A purple fringed scarf, shot through with silver threads, hung over the back of Saskia's chair. Absentmindedly Carolyn picked it up and shook it out, releasing a scent from the fabric – a spicy accretion of lemon, patchouli, sandalwood and smoke. Saskia's smell, as particular and unique as a fingerprint on the still air of the barn. Gently but firmly Carolyn folded the scarf and put it away in a drawer.

Her invitation that evening was from the Cunninghams, at the Old Rectory. Claire and Tom were a whisker younger than the Summerbys, with children at boarding school. Carolyn had long since realized that their childlessness made their social life less age-specific, if you weren't attached by offspring to the education ladder you were in some sense forever young.

The evening had been billed by Claire on the phone as 'kitchen supper'. Carolyn understood this was because she would be attending on her own, and a lone female introduced a note of informality. In Stoke Hetheridge even numbers were still de rigueur for a formal dinner party.

The other guests, as it turned out, were Rob and Angela Gorringe.

'What have you done with him?' asked Angela over the g and t's.

'He's in New York until the middle of next week.'

'Oh but surely he didn't have to go at the weekend!'

'He was going to see a few people today, and then have a New York Sunday. It's what he likes.'

'So why didn't you go?'

'I've got things to do here,' said Carolyn. Really, Angela could be a very trying woman. 'And we're going away together next month anyway.'

'Ah, yes,' said Rob. 'The anniversary! We're looking forward to your bash.'

'Claire!' called Angela. 'Are you all right out there?'

'Yes, thank you, shan't be long!'

'Smells delish...'

'It's fish pie,' said Tom. 'One of our specials, hope you like it.'

'Perfect,' said Carolyn.

Rob Gorringe leaned across confidingly.

'We owe you a debt of thanks.'

'You do? For what?'

'Employing our daughter.'

'Rob – you make it sound like some ghastly trial or sacrifice. She's a lovely girl.'

'She's a source of constant worry.'

'That's perfectly proper,' said Carolyn. 'You're her father. If she didn't worry you, and you weren't worried, something would be seriously wrong.'

'Anyway, we take considerable comfort from knowing she's suitably employed and safely occupied at the hall.'

There was one of those lulls in the conversation which Carolyn, who had a heightened sense of social responsibility, felt compelled to fill.

'So what's Saskia doing with herself this weekend?' she asked, including Angela in the question. 'There isn't a lot around here for the young.'

'That's why they drink so much,' said Tom, rising to his feet, bottle in hand. 'Top up?'

'She's in London,' said Angela. 'Staying with a college friend.'

Tom covered Carolyn's hand with his own as he filled her glass. 'Oops – steady, and it's only your second!'

'Due back tonight,' said Rob. 'Angie's the

non-drinker so she's on station fatigues.'

Angela grimaced. 'I told her it had to be the eleven o'clock, if she arrives home before midnight she can start walking.'

'That doesn't bother you?' asked Tom.

'Good grief!' Rob gave an incredulous grin. 'Have you seen our daughter? Anyone who tangled with her would get a lot more than he bargained for.'

Carolyn had now regrouped sufficiently to smile, and said, 'Good practice for South America.'

'Oh!' cried Angela. 'Don't start us on that!'

When Carolyn got back there was an email from Oliver. He had a room overlooking the park and though it was only five he was already sipping a dry martini to get him in a New York frame of mind. It went without saying (he said) that he would rather be sipping it with her, but you couldn't have everything. He hoped she had what he described as a 'jolly evening', and would try to speak to her when the first natural break occurred.

She sent a reply: Good night, all my love, Cx

Then she switched off and went to bed, where she lay still and rigid with her mind racing round and round like a hamster on a wheel.

On Monday morning Angela Gorringe rang Carolyn at the barn.

'Generally speaking she has the constitution of an ox, but she's very cheap today, and I'm prescribing bed and fluids of the non-toxic variety. Though for once,' added Angela forcefully, 'I'm not suggesting this is brewer's flu, it has all the hallmarks of the real deal, as they say.'

'I'm so sorry,' said Carolyn. 'Do give her my love, and tell her not to rush back till she's properly better.'

'I will.'

'And by the way, she left a nice scarf here, purple and silver. She might think she's lost it – tell her it's quite safe.'

'Bless you.'

Oliver was due back on the red-eye on Thursday morning. Carolyn sent a get-well card to Saskia, but saw nothing of her until late Wednesday afternoon, when she was tidying up preparatory to closing Top Notch for the day. The pea-green DCV rattled down the drive and lurched to a halt outside the front of the barn. There was a pause before Saskia emerged: Carolyn saw that she was finishing a cigarette, which she stubbed out in a tin-lid before getting out. She did in fact look a little under the weather, her peakiness emphasized by over-sized black clothes, in this case cargo pants, singlet and a baggy shirt.

Carolyn opened the door, and greeted her.

'Saskia, welcome! How are you, are you better?'

'Yes thanks.'

'I was just about to lock up here – come over to the house and have a glass of wine.'

'No, actually – no thanks.'

'All right, in that case come in.'

Saskia entered. Carolyn had turned off the music and the barn seemed very large and still, its high, timbered roof like the nave of a church – an old building that had been standing here quietly for nearly three hundred years.

'Tea?' asked Carolyn.

'No thanks.'

Saskia went over to her table, which was still pushed back as Carolyn had left it.

'Mum said I left a scarf here.'

'You did, it's in the top drawer.'

Saskia took out the scarf and held it clasped beneath folded arms as if it were a hot water bottle.

'Thanks.'

'Well—'

'Carolyn—'

They'd begun to speak at the same time. Carolyn said: 'You first.'

'I feel awful about this...'

'About what? I'm sure there's no need.'

'The thing is, I want to leave.'

Carolyn smiled. 'That's all right, I always knew you were going to.'

'No, I know, I mean I want to leave now.'

'Oh,' said Carolyn. 'Well, what can I say? I'll miss you.'

'I'm really, really sorry!' Relieved that there wasn't going to be a scene, the colour was returning to Saskia's cheeks. 'I feel really bad letting you down.'

'Don't. It doesn't matter. I've been lucky to have you and it was only ever an informal arrangement. Did something come up?'

'Yes – yes, I've got an offer of some free-lance work which I'd really like to do, and then if I can I want to leave for Peru in about a month.'

'That all sounds marvellous.'

'You're such a star, Carolyn.' Saskia's eyes shone with tears. 'You've been so good to me.'

'We've been good for each other.'

Saskia tipped her head back, taking in the whole of the barn, the great unused overhead expanse of it. 'This is such an incredible place.'

'Well, you know you're welcome back any time.'

'Thank you. Thank you.' Impulsively, Saskia came over and put her arms round Carolyn, kissing her on the cheek and laying her head on her shoulder. Carolyn felt the sprung vitality of that strong young body against hers, the buoyancy of the flesh, the smoothness of the skin, that distinctive smoky scent ... She placed her own hands lightly on Saskia's back, enclosing but not enfolding her.

'Come on, no tears. Brave and calm.'

'I feel such a louse.'

'You're not a louse.' Carolyn pushed her away and smiled at her, her hands on her shoulders. 'You're off on the great adventure.'

Saskia returned her smile with a slightly watery one. 'I hope so.'

'Of course you are.' Carolyn gave her a little shake. 'And I shall expect to hear all about it!'

The young have a quick emotional metabolism. Relief and gratitude came hard on the heels of tension and trepidation, and were usurped just as swiftly by the urge to escape. Two minutes later the DCV was jolting away up the drive and there was nothing left of Saskia but her scent, and a small damp patch on Carolyn's shoulder.

Carolyn realized that she had known this would happen. For now, she was calm; but the implications of Saskia's abrupt departure smudged the horizon like an enemy fleet – still distant, but ominous, and impossible to ignore.

Oliver got home at nine the next morning, looking remarkably fresh after his business-class flight, and bearing a flagon of designer scent entitled Femme du Monde.

Carolyn exclaimed with pleasure as she dabbed it behind her ears, on the hollow in her throat, the inside of her wrists.

'Is that what I am then?' she asked. 'A woman of the world?'

'You're the woman of my world.' He kissed her amorously. 'The only one.'

That evening, over drinks, she told him that Saskia had left. She didn't look at him as she told him, but she listened very carefully to the unspoken part of his reply.

'Has she? Why's that? Did you lock her in the broom cupboard once too often?'

'Something better came up, which I perfectly understand.'

'Bit peremptory, I'd have thought.'

'No – no, she wasn't. She was perfectly apologetic and nice about it. I don't mind.'

'I thought she was a bit of an asset.'

'She was, but I'll find someone else.' Carolyn rose to go into the kitchen. 'She was in London at the weekend, with a friend. It may have something to do with that.'

'Shouldn't be surprised,' said Oliver. 'The young are fickle.'

The next day Oliver worked at home, strolling across to his office in a blue shirt and chinos, and immediately getting on the phone. Carolyn put a wash on before going over to Top Notch. The white shirt with the very thin navy stripe, the one he'd worn when he went away last week, she left till last, touching it briefly to her face, inhaling, before pushing it into the round black 'O' of the machine.

Mrs Giorgescu would have liked her to try the dress on one last time, but she declined.

'I know it's going to be fine,' she said, as she wrote the cheque.

Mrs Giorgescu looped a carrier bag on to the hanger. 'I put the spare pieces in there – for when you get fat!'

She was still chuckling about this as she saw Carolyn out.

* * *

At the Summerbys' anniversary party it was generally agreed that Carolyn had never looked more beautiful, or more elegant. Not many women of a certain age could still wear basic black, but she was the exception. With her hair newly streaked, and a fresh dusting of diamonds, courtesy of Oliver, she was the toast of Stoke Hetherington, the magnet for every eye.

She had never had children, of course, which helped. Her figure had not been subjected to the attrition of child-bearing and raising, and let's face it, there were a whole slew of worries which she would never experience. When Claire complimented her on her appearance, and said it was her birthday coming up, Carolyn told her she had an unworn hand-made silk satin dress in the cupboard which didn't suit her, and that if Claire was interested she could have it.

No, she said, she wanted nothing for it. It would be nice to think of the dress having a life, instead of just hanging there. If Claire had no further use for it, or it didn't suit, she could always take it to Exchange and Smart.

'You'd be doing me a favour,' she said. 'It was never me, really.'

Monica

In my view, if you're known as a rebel, you have a duty to maintain your reputation, and live up to it. If you don't, you're sunk, because the alternative's just too dire. Think of all those hard alternative comedians – mentioning no names – who started out biting the heads off hecklers in the bear-pit clubs of the north, and wound up wearing Armani and having brunch with New Labour politicians. There's no sadder sight than a wild man – or woman – brought to heel by success: the mad grin replaced by an ingratiating smirk, the feral odour by Calvin Klein, the unkempt locks scrunch-dried by the crimper du jour, the fiery spirit set aside in favour of a pallid new-world white ... It makes my gorge rise.

Not that success is going to be my undoing. I'll remain uncorrupted in that regard, because it ain't going to happen. Success, I mean. Or not in the sense that everyone else means.

I leave all that to my younger sister Rosie, who apart from being an all-round good egg whom everyone likes (the sort of girl that both men and women refer to as 'a sweetie'), has already, at the age of thirty-five, ticked all the boxes: took a first in law at Durham; is a successful barrister in the family division; married an amusing man; borne two sparky and attractive children; continues to practise with the aid of a (mercifully plain) Slovenian au pair, and manages to be our parents' favourite and my closest confidante – not an easy trick to pull off, I assure you.

We girls were named after our grand-mothers, but I drew the short straw. Rose is a timeless classic – simple, lovely, fragrant – but be honest, how many Monicas under seventy do you come across? And while Rose is one of those names of which the diminutive is actually longer and sweeter than the original, when it comes to Monica, what are you going to do? At primary school I was Monkey; at secondary school, Mozzer, both of which sound like petty criminals. It's no wonder I'm anti-establishment.

What is astonishing is that Rosie and I have remained so close. In the Psychiatrist's Handbook we'd be the top case study for sibling rivalry and potential fratricide. I think I can take at least some of the credit, for realizing early on that I was in a no-contest situation, and heading rapidly in the opposite direction. I was the tough, trouble-some, non-academic older sister whom Rosie inexplicably worshipped. If she faced even a hint of bother, I sorted it out. I took the flack, and the rap, and took my punish-ments like a man. My hero was the Steve McQueen character in *The Great Escape* – banged up in the cooler yet again, laconi-cally, endlessly, smacking his baseball into the wall and catching it, not giving his captors the satisfaction. I may not have shone in the classroom, but I gave great dumb insolence.

I left school straight after GCSEs – four spoiled papers and a B in English – and went to work in a garden centre. The people who ran it were broad-minded, and I was safely deployed fetching and carrying in the outer reaches where my Edward Scissor-hands appearance wouldn't frighten the customers. At that stage I was a Goth, the full black-everything, clothes, hair, lips, nails, and so covered in metal I nearly sent airport security into meltdown when I went to Amsterdam for the weekend for a Waking Dead gig.

I went on my own to that. I was a loner.

Don't get me wrong, I could have had friends, but I didn't try. Respect was more important to me than friendship. To have friends would be to admit to needing people, to be one of the herd, and it was essential to my self-esteem not to do that. After the garden centre I went travelling, by the time I came back Rosie had her degree, and I got a job helping in a young people's care home. The Goth-ness had worn off – there are parts of the world where that look can get you thrown into the equivalent of Sing-Sing for the duration – and I just looked what I was, a stroppy, crop-headed, worked-out girl whom everyone assumed was gay. The kids in the house gave me no grief whatsoever.

Not so my parents. I haven't told you about them. Bronwyn and Clive, the nicest couple anyone knows, pillars of the community, wonderful hosts, supporters of charities, organizers of quiz nights and sponsored walks, members of U3A with a special interest in local history and archaeology ... I could go on, but it would make them sound insufferable. Which they were not, actually. I may have despised everything they stood for, but there was no getting away from the fact that our parents were good people.

I think they almost wanted me to be gay. They longed to embrace my issues, take them on, stand shoulder to shoulder with me in my differentness, stand up and be counted among all their pleasant, liberal lite, left-of-centre friends. Bronwyn and Clive – the only ones to have their principles tested and come through with flying colours! Every time I went there I saw the looks of deep, supportive understanding on their faces, just below the surface, waiting for the news. But I couldn't oblige.

You see, I had a dark secret.

I wanted to fall in love. Not with a woman, either. Nor with some lily-livered metro-sexual with more hair product than hormones. No, I wanted some great, hairy-arsed, testosterone-fuelled bloke to sweep me off my feet and all the way to the altar – the registrar, anyway. Or if not that, at least to passionate cohabitation with a view to procreation. My parents would have been astonished if they knew the fantasies that disturbed my sleep. Where, I asked myself, were all the unreconstructed pre-feminist he-men when you needed them? After all, it wasn't the swooning, marble-skinned lovelies who needed to be tossed over someone's shoulder and carried off into the night. They'd have – well – swooned. No, it was us stroppy, attitude-toting tomboys who needed it. We were the challenge, dammit, so where were the champions? I went with Rosie and the kids to see The Taming of the Shrew (Ellie was doing it for GCSE) and was restless for weeks afterwards. Where was the Petruchio to my Kate? I'd built up the biggest defences in the history of the sex war, was there no one man enough to breach them?

No, came the answer: not in this town.

When it came to my sexuality, my parents didn't so much tiptoe around the subject as sit watching quietly, just out of range, with an air of gentle patience and understanding like a couple of horse whisperers befriending a mustang.

My mother is what's known as a man's woman, from the crown of her feathery coiffure to the tip of her glossy pedicure. She was just dying to tell me my appearance didn't matter a jot to her, so I always pushed my luck, wearing blasphemous T-shirts and combats so low-rise they barely covered my pubes. The last conversation I had with her was when she and Dad had Rosie's youngest, Johnny, to stay and I'd taken him to the pictures to give them a break. He was a tall twelve and I'd curried favour shamelessly by taking him to a Cert 15 gore-fest called The Black Hole about mutants who lived in the sewers, and were sufficiently adaptable to slither up the drains and drag unsuspecting victims round the U-bend or even – ingenious this – down the plughole, using their long, whiplike tentacles, razor-edged to slice through metal and flesh. It was pretty fair, though as usual the build-up was a lot more scary than the extended and messy climax. A camera with a mutant's-eye-view moving, Jaws-like, along the pipe towards some wretched unprotected backside really tightens the sphincter; I didn't have a decent dump for days. But once the carnage got underway there was nowhere left to go and it got tedious.

Anyway, Johnny liked it. Out of Rosie's two he's the one with a bit of an Asboid tendency, and he thinks I'm quite cool, so we're reasonably bonded. I delivered him back to his grandparents at about eight, having rounded things off with an all-day-breakfast pizza and wedges, and I would have zoomed off into the night but my mother appeared and waved me to come in.

'Good film?' she asked Johnny.

'Yeh, it was well cool.'

'Is it something Pops and I should go and see?'

Johnny caught my eye and I'm afraid we both smirked. 'Er – no.'

'All right, I shan't ask,' said my mother. 'Have you eaten, because—?'

'We had pizza,' I interupted.

'Can I go on the computer?' asked Johnny.

'Yes, as long as you leave everything as you found it.'

Johnny disappeared upstairs. 'Where's Dad?' I asked.

'Summer show committee meeting. He's only just gone. Come and sit down. Glass of wine? Coffee?'

'No, I'm fine, thanks.'

'Sit down anyway, it's ages since I saw you to talk to.'

Mum placed considerable weight on this 'seeing to talk to' thing. I suppose it was her version of the dreaded 'quality time', something I strenuously avoided. But there was no escape. She had a glass of sauvignon on the go, and Cool Classics in the background, she was well up for it.

I went into the clean, comfy lounge with its archaeological books on the coffee table and its book-club choices on the shelves, and slid into the armchair that was within sight of the door. My mother turned the music down a couple of notches and sat down on the sofa with the very special

68

welcoming smile she reserved for her prodigal daughter.

'Thank you so much, darling, for taking Johnny out. We do love having him, but it's nice to have a break, not to mention the food aspect, he's going through that fridge-emptying stage, I can't keep pace with it!'

'Don't worry, he's well stocked up.'

'How are you? How's work?'

'It's good.'

'Not on nights at the moment?'

'Next week.'

She chuckled at some memory. 'And no more hideous incidents, I hope?'

'No. Well – stuff happens, they're very troubled kids, but nothing life-threatening.'

'God...' She shook her head, eyes closed. 'I don't know. It just makes me realize how lucky we are. Fridge raiding notwithstanding!'

'Oh,' I said, 'they do that, too. Carbs are the answer. We have more cheap white bread and cornflakes in that place than you can imagine.'

'What if one of them has a gluten allergy?'

'That's not allowed.'

She chuckled again, thinking I was joking.

'And what about you?' she asked. 'Are you looking after yourself in all this?'

'Naturally.'

Her eyes were fixed on my face like twin lasers. 'Managing to have some fun, or is it all work, work, work?'

'Mum.'

'What?'

'It's not all work.'

'I'm very pleased to hear it.'

She'd get no more out of me, and she knew it. We were both wily customers, used to each other's tactics.

Rosie was more successful, if only because she was more direct, and was peddling no agenda. A few weeks after The Black Hole she and I met for a drink between her work and my night shift. Generally speaking she liked to be home in the early evening, to crack the whip over homework, cook a nourishing supper and massage Julian's feet or whatever they got up to. But once a month we got together like this, away from our respective responsibilities. We alternated between her wine bar, the Vintage, and my local, the Blacksmiths Arms. Tonight it was my turn. Not that the pub had seen a blacksmith, or any kind of honest trades-person, for centuries – unless you counted pushers, pimps and the like. I exaggerate slightly, but you get the picture. The Blacksmiths Arms was a place where the pitbull was the pet of choice.

It goes without saying that of the two of us Rosie – in her natty black trouser suit and little gold specs – stood out a lot more than me. There were special hooks under the tables to hang bags on so they didn't get nicked, and I always made sure Rosie put her briefcase on one.

In my pub I'm in the chair, so I got in our usuals – a half of Hellraiser for me, a long vodka tonic for her, and a packet of barbecue-flavour crisps. Because Rosie's been coming in five or six times a year for about ten years they've just about mastered how she likes the v and t – tall glass, third full of ice, slice of lime, single shot of vodka, one tonic in and the other on the side – but the barman still managed to give the impression he's involved in some complex and potentially dangerous scientific experiment.

'Cheers,' said Rosie when I get back. 'And thanks again for taking Johnny out.'

'It was my pleasure. He and I get on fine.'

'Yes, I forget – you're a practised hand with the hooded young.'

'You could say that.'

'How are the little buggers?'

'We had an arson attempt the other night.'

'Jesus! How successful, on a scale of one to ten?'

I thought about this. 'Six?'

71

'Actual flames, then?'

'Oh yes, Leaping, licking – we had to call the fire brigade.'

'But it was all okay in the end?'

'Yes. Garden shed's a goner, but we were insured.'

'Thank heavens, it must have been full of stuff.'

'Yup.' I pulled a face. 'All the gardening equipment we're devastated to see the back of, plus those healthy outdoor games they can't bear to be without – badminton, bat and ball, croquet—'

Rosie shrieked. 'Croquet? Don't tell me you play croquet with them?'

'M-hmm. We turn the skinny ones upside down and use them as mallets.'

She hooted with laughter again. We were allowed to make jokes about the Troubled Young, because we both worked with them – like Jews telling stories against themselves.

'How about you?' I asked. 'Anything groundbreaking going on?'

'Not really, it's as depressing as ever. No one stays together and when they separate they rip each other to bits. If Julian ever gets a fancy piece I'll be stoical. It'd take a lot more than a bit on the side to drive me to divorce.'

'If he does, I'll kill him.'

She touched my hand and I glanced round – I wondered if the Blacksmiths Arms knew we were sisters.

'You would too. Tell me, how were the Ps when you saw them?'

'I only saw Mum. Dad was out doing his bit somewhere. She was in sparkling form.'

Rosie detected the slight gritting of teeth that accompanied this report. 'Being a concerned parent, huh? As a matter of fact, don't knock it.'

'I don't, I'm used to it.'

'You know,' said Rosie, 'if you actually told them something now and again, I mean actually volunteered something as opposed to playing the closed book, they might back off. Throw a bone to them, give them something to chew on.'

'I can't be bothered.'

'You're so pathologically reticent, Mon! It doesn't matter what you tell them, it can be a pack of lies if you like, but everyone would be happy.'

'I can't stand it – she's just dying to be understanding, they both are.'

'Doesn't everyone want to be understood?' mused Rosie. 'It's like love, surely they do...'

'Not me,' I said. 'I want to be left alone.'

Rosie didn't pursue it because, unlike the

parents, she genuinely does understand me, knows the value I place on my privacy, and makes no big deal of it.

But even I can see I'm pretty pathological. I mean I had an opening there to tell her about the fireman, and I didn't. Even though it would have made her day, and she would never have breathed a word, even to Julian, I said nothing.

I know, I know, firemen are a cliché. They have a calendar, my mother's hairdresser has one hanging by the reception area. It's a unisex hairdresser, and I've often wondered if male customers are offended by it as much as we women used to be by the pin-ups in the local tyre and exhaust centre before the new management introduced a carpeted area with a playpen, a telly and a coffee machine.

This one, the one I'm talking about, I later found out was called Fergal – bit of a gay name, in the way kids use the term, imprecisely, as one of general mild disparagement. Gay he certainly wasn't. The phrase 'giant of a man' springs to mind. I was standing in the garden in my pyjamas and after he and his colleagues put out the last of the flames and the other two were rolling up the hose and stowing it on the fire

74

engine, he came stomping over in his big wellies to fill me in on the damage.

'Don't go near it for twenty-four hours, miss, and be careful when you do. I'm afraid whatever was in there's a goner.'

'Toerag,' I said.

Fortunately he knew who I was referring to. 'You got a few of them in this place, I bet.'

'Goes with the territory.'

'Course it does.'

He towered over me, smelling of soot, rubber and honest sweat. There was something massively reassuring about him, I was sure he could have handled any situation, not just because of his size but because of his air of calm authority. This, I reckoned, was not only a man who would never have been bullied at school, but would have protected the ones who were. He took off his gloves and I had a sudden insight into why some people like to watch strippers – there is something sexy about the uncovering of flesh. Apart from his smoke-blackened face his hands were the only exposed part of his body, and of course they were clean; spotless. I couldn't take my eyes off them – enormous hands, like shovels, with pronounced knuckles and joints, and thick veins on the back ... I'm embarrassed to admit this, but my heart actually beat faster.

Adrian, our team leader, had been inside with Meriel, keeping order and ensuring none of our tender charges took the opportunity of all this excitement to ransack the place or run away. There were faces at every window. Now he emerged from the back door and came over.

'All under control?' he asked.

'Yup. Could have been worse. Thank your lucky stars he didn't torch the house.'

'Or she.'

'Equal opportunities,' agreed the fireman. I had the impression this might have been a gentle dig.

'Anyway,' said Adrian, 'it was definitely started deliberately – in your opinion?'

'No question.'

'How can you be so sure?'

'Well for a start...'

I watched as Adrian listened intently to the explanation. Adrian has a prissy manner and one of those beard-and-moustache combos which might have caused a more prejudiced person to wonder if his interest was of a personal nature. For some reason I felt quite irritated. Fortunately the exchange was brought to a halt when the two other firemen came back round the corner, an upstairs window opened and Jodie Lopez leaned out.

'Hey, guys, get yer kit off!'

'Jodie! Cut that out! Sorry, officer,' said Adrian.

'Don't worry, we get it all the time.'

'I'm going to put the kettle on,' I said. 'How about a brew?'

He consulted his watch, which looked built to withstand not only fire, but flood, earthquake and very probably pestilence too.

'Go on then,' he said. 'Thanks. Be with you in a minute.'

He went to talk to the other two and Adrian fell in beside me. 'Is that such a good idea?' he hissed. 'You heard Jodie. The sooner we can lower the temperature the better.'

'For God's sake,' I snapped, 'it's only a cup of tea.'

Only a cup of tea? Er – no.

I may have looked like a woman who was putting out mugs, applying water to tea bags and retrieving the best biscuits from the sealed jar at the back of the staff-supply cupboard, but my world was shifting on its axis. Not that I wanted to admit it, and my uncharacteristic self-consciousness made me even brusquer than usual.

Adrian didn't want tea, and swapped with Meriel, going to keep an eye on the kids while she came to join us in the kitchen. Meriel is in her twenties and pretty, with long hair and a peasant skirt. When she came in I sensed that small but noticeable change in the air that means the pheromones are flying around. Nothing overt, just a tiny sonar beep of woman-awareness. Mainly from the other two blokes, to be fair.

'Everything under control?' asked my one.

'As much as it ever is – eh, Mon?' said Meriel.

I made some non-committal sound, aware that I wasn't coming over well, but too pigheaded to do anything about it.

One of the others found his tongue. 'Any idea who started it?'

'Oh yes.' Meriel glanced at me again. 'Oh, yes.'

'They need watching.'

'We will. We do. Oh, wow, are those jammy dodgers? We must have fires more often.'

Fergal may have put out one fire, but he had started another, one which turned into an almighty conflagration. No matter how much I castigated myself for stupidity and told myself that this was a schoolgirl crush not matched since my David Essex phase, that it would pass and I'd get over it, the feeling didn't go away. I dreamed about him, he hovered on the edge of my consciousness the whole time. I was gripped by that sort of luxurious, sweet, toxic melancholy that you get when you're fourteen and believe the whole world's against you but you quite like it that way.

So when about three days later he turned up at the house again, I was completely thrown. It was a Saturday evening and I was in the kitchen helping Meriel make shepherd's pie. Adrian was in the office and Jodie Lopez answered the door, with predictable results which we couldn't help overhearing.

'Hey, aren't you the fire chief?'

'I was here the other night, yes.'

I ran a hand through my hair – it had been stubble but had progressed to chicken feathers – and hoped Meriel would attribute my high colour to the frying mince.

Jodie closed the door. I tried to remember what she was wearing today. A crop-top and a denim miniskirt, probably. I was in my usual voluminous combats and a Darkness T-shirt. I was also sweating profusely.

'If you smelt smoke, it's just them making tea,' said Jodie. She appeared in the kitchen doorway with Fergal at her shoulder.

'We got a visitor.'

'Hallo!' said Meriel. 'Thanks, Jodie.'

She sniffed. 'When are we eating?'

'Six o'clock,' I said in my steeliest voice. 'As usual.'

She made an 'Oooh!' face and withdrew.

'Don't know about the smoke,' said Fergal, 'but it smells good.'

'Want some?' asked Meriel. 'It'll be ready soon.'

'No, no ... I'm not stopping,' he said. 'I just dropped by to see how things were after the other night – it can be a messy business getting cleared up after a fire, even if it is only a shed.'

'We got a work party out there,' I said, then added boldly: 'You'd have been proud of us.'

'Good for you. Mind if I take a peep?' he asked. 'There are odd things to look out for, might help us nail the perpetrator.'

'Don't worry,' said Meriel. 'His social worker and the police have already been round.'

'Glad to hear it. But if you don't mind I'll take a butcher's anyway.' He looked at me. 'You were out there when we arrived, weren't you?'

'Yes,' I laid down my spatula. 'I'll show you.'

I took him into the garden. Two of the lads

were out on the patio, playing cards. They didn't so much as glance at us, but I knew our presence – especially his – had been registered, and not favourably. Out of uniform my companion looked remarkably like an off-duty policeman.

There was a large black patch on the grass where the shed had been, and the least-damaged planks and timbers were stacked in the centre under a tarpaulin. Surviving metal objects – the lawn-mower, the barbecue, tent pegs – stood to one side like the blackened bones of strange beasts. Even now there was a faint smell of smoke and charring in the air, and as we drew closer the ground still seemed to be giving off heat.

'All very neat and tidy,' he said.

I watched as he conducted a brief survey of the area, peering closely, occasionally nudging at the ground with the toe of his shoe, and once stooping to pick up some small object before examining and discarding it. Another time he crouched down for closer inspection, squatting on his heels in an attitude which showed off the extreme muscularity of his thighs.

'Okay,' he said at last. 'Good job.'

I felt as if I'd won some major award.

Instead of heading back to the house he stood next to me, facing away from it (and away from the lads, whose ears must have been flapping under their hoods), his hands in his pockets, as though we were admiring some splendid view instead of the sooty remains of an old shed. I folded my arms, felt awkward like that, and tucked my hands into my hip pockets instead.

'You're busy then,' he said.

'It's that time of day.'

'How many you got here?'

'Eight at the moment. Never more than ten.'

'Rather you than me.'

'It's okay.'

'Oh yeah, don't get me wrong, good work – that's what I mean really. No kidding, I'd rather deal with a fire at a petro-chemical plant than do your job.'

I said: 'We won't swap then.'

We were neither of us looking at each other. He bent down with great concentration and picked a daisy, which he twiddled between his fingers.

'When do you get off?' he asked.

I wasn't quite sure I'd heard him. 'Sorry?'

'When do you finish work?'

'Tomorrow morning, nine o'clock.'

He gave a short laugh. 'Silly question.'

'Unsocial hours.'

'Me too.'

'Price we pay for being in the caring professions.'

'You reckon.'

There was an awkward silence during which I wondered if he was going to follow up the original question or just leave it at that.

'Right—'

'Okay—'

'After you,' I said.

'Wondered if you might fancy a drink some time.'

'With you?'

For the first time he turned and looked at me. Stared, in fact. I was still gazing at the shed, but I felt the stare which was intended to make me feel a prat and succeeded.

'No,' he said, 'with Dr Who. Of course with me.'

'Sorry,' I said and then added, echoing him as pointedly as I dared: 'Silly question.'

'Is that a yes?'

'OK.'

'Wednesday evening any good?'

'Sure.' I was acting casual, but inside I was in uproar.

'Do you know the Box Tree in Waverley Road?'

'I think so.'

'Yeah?' He'd decided not to trust me and

was checking.

'I'll find it.'

'Course you will. Eight o'clockish suit you?'

'Fine.'

'Good job.' So that was just an expression, not a compliment – never mind. He took his hands out of his pockets and turned towards the house. 'See you then. Look forward to it.'

I saw Adrian in the kitchen, looking out. He held up a hand to detain us, but I pretended I hadn't seen.

'No need to go back through,' I said. 'We can go round the side.'

The two lads had abandoned their card game and were lying on their stomachs like a couple of prisoners awaiting brutal interrogation.

Neither of them looked up, but one of them said, 'All right, miss?'

It wasn't a question that required an answer, he was just letting me know they knew what I was up to – whatever that was.

'Rather you than me,' said my companion for a second time.

Needless to say Adrian wasn't so easily brushed off when he perceived his authority to be at stake. He cut us off at the pass and was waiting in the drive.

'Evening, officer. Any problems?'

'No, routine visit.'

'I never realized the fire service provided aftercare,' said Adrian in his slightly waspish manner.

'I was just passing.'

'And Monica's been looking after you?'

Fuck.

'Yes she has. Right, I'll clear off and let you have your tea. Cheerio. Bye, Monica.'

It occurred to me that it was just possible he didn't find my name funny.

Anyway he was way ahead of me – I didn't even know his.

'Fergal Docherty.'

No wonder he hadn't reacted, he had a silly name too.

'Is this your local?'

'You're joking – that's no place for a lady.'

Did he mean me?

'No need to worry,' I said, 'you should see mine.'

'Where's that?'

'The Blacksmith's Arms in Chalcot Street.'

'You win.'

For some reason I sprang to the Blacksmith's defence. 'It's not as bad as all that. I take my sister there and she's a barrister.'

'That doesn't prove anything. Briefs have to mix with low-lifes, it goes with the job.'

'She's in the family division.'

'I rest my case.'

Congratulating myself on my subtlety, I said: 'That's a bit harsh. I don't have a family myself, but Rosie's is very nice.'

'Me neither.'

That cleared one thing up, but the main elephant was still there.

'And she and her husband have been married eighteen years and still like each other.'

'Fair play,' said Fergal. 'I only managed three years, and two of those were out and out war.'

'I'm sorry,' I said, because it was what people said in films. Actually my heart leapt at the news.

'It was a long time ago. We're friends now.'

Damn. 'That's good.'

'She married again. I think he's a prize twat, but it's not my opinion that matters.'

'No.'

We thought about this. We were sitting not at a table but at the bar like a couple of old regulars and I was trying to tell myself that this was not after all a date, but a drink with a bloke who had seen what so many people seem to see in me – a kind of honorary other bloke.

He might not have realized this, but I had made what constituted a major effort in my book. I was wearing my black charity-shop trousers – the ones I'd got for accompanying kids to court – with the blue polo-shirt I sometimes wore to the gym. It was clean, and had no writing on it. I rather despised myself for pretending – or seeming to pretend – to be something I wasn't, but justified it on the grounds that he'd seen my day-to-day appearance and it hadn't put him off.

He was wearing a plaid work-shirt, jeans and timberlands. Real men's clothes of the sort that can easily be taken as a very different signal, but not in his case. He was drinking the local bitter, I was on the Hell-raiser.

He nodded at my glass. 'That your usual then?'

'It is, yes,' I said, and hearing the defensive note in my voice added: 'It's good stuff, pity about the name.'

'Thought you might have chosen it because of that,' he said.

'Why would I do that?'

'I don't know. Let's just say you don't look like a chardonnay girl.'

Now what did that mean? I certainly

strove not to look like a 'chardonnay girl', but would his interpretation be the same as mine?

'Thank you,' I said.

He smiled. There followed another quasi-blokey silence, which he broke.

'Monica. What's all that about?'

Fuck and double-fuck.

'Sorry?'

I was looking daggers, but he was all smiles. 'It's a fine old-fashioned moniker, Monica. Were you named after your grandma?'

'Yes, as it happens.'

'Bet you're glad she wasn't called Ethel.'

I chose not to dignify this with a reply.

'And your other grandma was called Rose.'

'How did you guess?'

I was being sarcastic, but he either didn't notice or didn't care.

'Your sister.'

'Correct.'

He took a swig of his beer, saying, as he raised his glass: 'Would you want to be called Rose?'

He'd got me there. 'No.'

'There you are then,' he said matter of factly, as if he'd proved the point.

I suffered one of those plummeting dips in

morale that happen sometimes, which make you just wish you could be spirited away from wherever you are. Or alternatively start all over again. I felt both comfortable and uncomfortable with him. This was because I felt – let's see – known. Which could have been good or bad.

I told myself to get a grip. I was old enough and ugly enough to handle this, and I would. All I had to do was make small-talk for another, what, twenty minutes or so, and I could decently make my excuses and leave.

'What about you?'

'I've got a sister too. Maureen. She lives in Leicester.'

'What does she do?'

'She's a dental nurse.'

I couldn't think of a thing to say about this, but fortunately another route opened up.

'Are you Irish?'

'You'd think so, wouldn't you?' he said affably. 'There must have been some Irish blood swilling about on my dad's side a few generations back, but none that's around now.'

'So what's with the Fergal and Maureen?' I asked caustically, paying him back for the Monica dig.

'They go well with Docherty?' He was saying he didn't know the answer, but this was an educated guess.

I felt pretty stupid, but I ploughed on. Interrogating him was preferable to the alternative.

'Are your parents still alive?'

'My dad is. He lives here, not far from me.'

'Do you get on?'

'Oh yeah, he's the bollocks. I love him to bits.'

The straightforwardness of this quite took my breath away and before I could stop myself I said: 'Lucky you.'

'He's not too clever these days – arthritis and whatever – but he's good company. I go round there a lot. Rustle up a bit of grub, have a few beers, watch the footie...' He smiled to himself. 'Yours around?'

'Yes. Both of them.' Thinking of my parents made me realize that I might rather unfairly have given the impression they and I were at each other's throats. 'They're okay really.'

'Good as that, eh?'

'No, they are. They're very – active.'

'See much of them?'

'Now and again. My sister does more because of the kids. But we get on fine – you know.'

It was then that Fergal did something very tactful, and tact's a kind of grace, isn't it? A much more noble and valuable quality than it's given credit for.

'I tell you what,' he said. 'My old man nags.'

'Does he?' My voice rose a couple of semitones with relief.

'Oh, yeah. He means well, but he doesn't half bang on.'

'What about?'

'About me being single. It worries him, don't know why. Or at least I do, he's old fashioned and he thinks a man can't be happy without the love of a good woman.'

'Mine do that.'

He gave a short, humorous sigh. 'They're all the same.'

'What about you?' I asked. 'What do you think?'

'About what?'

'Can a man be happy on his own?'

'You bet. Look at me.' He held out his arms and I looked. 'Clean shirt, full belly, steady income. A model citizen. And all without a good woman.'

'Modest, too.'

'Right.' He laughed. 'Tell you what though.'

'What?'

'Wouldn't say no to a bad one.'

We met again the following week, this time at the Blacksmith's. Here, sitting at the bar was strictly for the dealers and scorers, so we were at a table near the window. Just outside sat a large brown dog, tied to the down-pipe.

'Surprised he doesn't get stolen round here,' said Fergal.

'I'm not,' I said. 'You'd have to be suicidal. He's a Rhodesian Ridgeback.'

'Not heard of those.'

'Like a pitbull but without the cuddly charm.'

'Stone me...' Fergal studied the dog with a new respect. 'I always thought I'd like a dog, but it'd be hopeless in my job.'

'Adrian's got one,' I said.

'Adrian?'

'My boss. Team leader at the care home.'

'What sort has he got?'

'Lhasa Apso.'

'If you say so.'

'Like a mop – two mops, you can't tell which way it's going.'

'Sounds a bit poofy.'

'Yes, but it's quite cute. The kids love it.'

He nodded, and leaned back with his arms

folded. He had broad shoulders and a big chest. I took a huge slurp of Hellraiser to quieten myself.

'So how do you get on with them?' he asked.

'The kids? They're okay. Anyway, they're all different. Just because they're in care doesn't make them all bastards.'

'That one who opened the door for me–'

'Jodie.'

'That Jodie. Bet she's a handful.'

'She's not so bad. Messed about by her father.'

'Scum,' said Fergal in his matter-of-fact voice.

'Fraid so.'

'Pretty girl, too. Ought to be playing netball and studying for her exams, not putting out for men old enough to be—Yeah, I get the picture. Scum,' he said again, and sighed heavily. I could have sworn his eyes were shining.

'Another half?' I suggested.

'No thanks. Tell you what.' He laid his hands palms down on the table and leaned forward. 'Do you like curry?'

We both knew the British Raj, and the young waiter in there smiled his big ivory smile at the coincidence of seeing us together. The Raj had been going for as long as either of us could remember, but there were never more than six people in there and tonight was no exception. We ordered poppadums, one chicken, two veg, a pilau rice, a stuffed piratha, and a couple of bottles of Cobra.

'I'm surprised we haven't seen each other in here before,' said Fergal.

'We probably have. Seen, but not noticed.'

'Oh no,' he said, 'I'd have noticed.'

I thought that was a compliment, but I still wasn't quite sure where he was coming from, so I ignored it. We hadn't touched, and I couldn't read the body language – not that I'm an expert.

My next drink with Rosie was at the Vintage Wine Bar. You can't get Hellraiser there, so I have one of their poncey overpriced designer lagers, so cold you can't taste it, and she has a large Merlot.

After the first swig she looked at me sideways.

'You look well, Mon.'

'Yes, I'm fine thanks.'

'No I mean well, well. As in – great.'

I looked down at myself – baggies and grey T-shirt. 'Really?'

'Not the clothes. You. What's going on?'

'Gee, thanks.'

'Come on, don't fence, you know what I mean.'

I had a moment's internal debate, and then decided that if I had to confide in anyone it might as well be the only person I could confide in, i.e. my sister. Still, I chose my words carefully.

'I'm seeing someone.'

'Good,' she said calmly. I bet she wasn't calm, I bet she was waving flags and whooping inside, but she had the sense not to show it. 'You want to tell me who?'

'Fergal,' I said. 'Fergal Docherty.'

'Good craic?'

'He's not Irish.'

'Silly me.'

'Or only way back, he's as English as you or me.'

'And you like him?' She couldn't help smiling. 'Don't you?'

'Yes,' I said, and the infectious smile spread to my face, too. 'I do.'

Rosie shook her head, still smiling, lips closed so that her cheeks dimpled. She closed her eyes for a second. When she opened them again they were dark and bright, full of her love for me.

'I am pleased, Mon.'

'Don't get your hopes up,' I said tartly.

'We've had a few pints and a couple of curries.'

'Do the Ps know?'

'There's nothing to know ... No, they don't.'

'They may guess. Mum, anyway. You look amazing.'

'I'll make a point of having a hangover when I next drop in.'

Rosie shook her head again, her eyes never left my face. 'What does Fergal do when he's not showing you a good time?'

'He's a fireman.'

'Mon!' She tipped her head back and laughed.

'What's so funny?'

'Nothing. No – a fireman?'

'Yes.'

'That is so sexy it's practically a cliché. But not, of course,' she added hastily.

'They're not all hunks,' I pointed out.

'But he is, I take it.'

'Well— ' the weasel smile wriggled out of the bag again – 'yes.'

'Mon!'

She got up, leaned over the table, grabbed my head and kissed me on the mouth – behaviour which would have turned every last shaven head in the Blacksmiths, but caused not an eyelid to bat in here. 'You little devil!'

When she sat down again my face was on fire and I spoke in a stage whisper: 'I told you, nothing's happened.'

'Best bit!' she said. 'It's a well-known fact, the best bit is the period leading up to the first kiss.'

She was wrong about that. The first kiss was just the start.

I didn't know I had it in me. Passion, tenderness, sensuality. Or perhaps I assumed it was all there but had squashed it down for so many years I was in denial. I needn't have worried. When, after no preamble, Fergal took me in his arms, it was like (excuse the incendiary metaphor) like throwing a match on dry twigs.

Up I went.

And the kiss seemed to free him up too, because afterwards he said all the things he should have said before. We were sitting in my car round the corner from the fire station and the gear lever – I think it was the gear lever – was in the way.

'Jesus, Monica, I fancy you.'

'Do you?'

'From the first moment I saw you.'

'Me too.'

'You're my fantasy woman.' He kissed me

again and I came up, reeling.

'Really?'

To prove it he thrust his big hand down the neck of my T-shirt and beneath my right breast. I'm pretty well-endowed in that department, but he could hold the lot and his hand was surprisingly gentle – as if he was holding a bird.

Rose was right. My mother spotted something immediately, and I knew she wouldn't have been told – my sister's discretion was watertight, with her own husband, let alone our parents.

The next time I went round it was a Saturday afternoon and both of them were in – or rather out, because they were gardening. They'd pretty much stopped inviting me round for Sunday lunches and whatnot, outside Christmas and birthdays, and relied on me to drop in, which suited both of us.

'Darling! What a lovely surprise!' My mother sat back on her heels, trowel in hand, and wiped a stray lock from her pink face with the wrist of her gardening glove. She was the only woman I knew who actually did, quite naturally, the things that actresses do in films, when they're playing charmingly natural.

'David!' she called to my father who was straddling the rockery with his backside in the air. 'Monica's here!'

'What?'

'Monica!'

'Well, hallo there!'

He straightened up a bit creakily – they were super-fit for their age but they always said gardening stiffened the parts other activities failed to touch – and came over. They both kissed me and declared they were ready for a break. My father set out the folding chairs and went in to fetch a jug of something and Mum and I sat down.

'So you've got a Saturday off,' she said. 'At last.'

She didn't have a clue about my schedule, but was fixated on the idea that I was overworked and never had time to myself.

'Right through till tomorrow night.'

'Anything planned?' she asked.

'Nothing much. Chilling out, catching up on some sleep.'

'As a matter of fact you're looking rather well,' she said in that slightly surprised tone she reserved for favourable comments about my appearance. I'm sure she didn't mean it to be insulting. Maybe she didn't realize she was doing it.

My father came round the corner with a

jug of lime squash with ice, mint and lime slices, and put it down on the folding table. My mother poured.

'So, how's life treating you?' he asked. He had a way with these global questions, which were so carefully non-specific I could only give the blandest and most formulaic of replies.

'Fine, thanks.'

'I was just saying she looks well,' said my mother, handing me my glass.

'She does. You do. How are things in the world of the disadvantaged young?'

'Busy – you know.'

'An ever-expanding market.'

'You could say that. Unfortunately.'

'I wish them no ill, but they are your living, after all.'

Dad's whole working life had been in commerce, and he had difficulty in seeing things any other way.

'I suppose.'

'Have you seen Rose recently?' asked my mother.

'We had our regular drink together.'

'And how was she?'

'Full of beans.' This wasn't one of my expressions, it was one of theirs. When in Rome.

'You know it's Tara's eighteenth next

month.'

I recalled something of the kind. 'She did mention it.'

'It falls on a Saturday, so they're having a family lunch and then a bash for her friends in the evening,' my mother told me. She took the view – usually correct – that when it came to information of this kind even if I had been told already I would probably have forgotten so she might as well ram the message home.

'You will come, won't you?' she asked, with the merest edge of anxiety.

'I expect so. I haven't been asked.'

This was ungracious, and got what it deserved.

'Monica. Of course you'll be asked. You'll be top of the list.'

'I'm sure I will.'

'I take it they let you change your shift at that place, if something pressing comes up,' asked my father.

'Naturally.'

My mother sighed happily. 'It should be lovely, they've booked Mendlesham Mill.'

Fergal and I couldn't keep our hands off each other. We usually went to his place rather than my flat which was tiny and always a mess. He had a two-up two-down terraced house that he kept astonishingly clean and tidy. The first time I went there I didn't really notice, we just fell on each other like ravening beasts and stayed in bed until I had to rush off for my night shift. The second time the pattern was much the same except I didn't have to rush off and he made supper afterwards. While he rustled up the stir-fry, shaking and tossing it like a pro, I had a look round and then came to sit at the kitchen table.

'Nice house,' I said.

'It's all right, isn't it?' he agreed. 'Bit small, but it suits me.'

'It's a palace next to my place.'

'Do you own yours?'

'No. Rent.'

'You're barmy girl,' he said affably, putting a plate in front of me and kissing my neck. 'You might as well flush the money down the toilet.'

'I don't earn much and I don't want to be saddled with a mortgage.'

'But you're saddled with rent, and it's going nowhere. Correction, it's going into the landlord's pocket.'

I ignored him and took a mouthful. 'This is great.'

'Part of my extensive repertoire – stew, stir-fry and spag bol. Oh, and I do a mean full English.'

'We do that for the kids at weekends,' I said.

'You can't beat it.' He had his plate now, but was sitting with his elbows on the table watching me eat. If anyone else had been doing that I'd have been embarrassed, but with him it felt almost as though I was giving him some wonderful present – which I suppose I was in a way, eating his delicious food with gusto.

'Tell you what I'd like,' he said.

'What's that?'

He gave his plate a little push as though setting it aside while he focused on something important.

'I'd like to make breakfast for you.'

I nodded round a mouthful. 'Sure. Any time.'

'No. I mean on a regular basis.'

I put down my fork. My stomach had got tight, suddenly. 'How regular?'

'Like ... let's see ... Every day?'

I couldn't believe what I was hearing, so with my usual suave fluency and legendary cool I said: 'You what?'

'I'm proposing, girl. And obviously not making much of a fist of it.'

'Proposing?'

'Yes. Marriage.'

'Us – get married?'

'It was just a thought. Take your time.'

'Thanks.' I took another leisurely mouthful, chewed, and swallowed. 'Okay.'

He gave me a sideways look, eyes narrowed, before asking cautiously:

'Is that a yes?'

'Yes, it's a yes.'

'Phew...' He pulled his plate back. 'Thank God that's out of the way.'

The best things in life are free, so we finished the stir-fry and celebrated in the best way possible.

'Yes.'

One little word and the world spun on its axis. As for those three little words that are supposed to be so indispensable to emotional commitment, up till then neither of us had actually uttered them. It hadn't seemed necessary.

Next morning in Fergal's bathroom mirror I studied my reflection for signs of the inner radiance which Rosie and my mother had commented on. I certainly looked no different in most respects. I was no one's idea (except, apparently, Fergal's) of a babe. My hair stuck up; I had broad, square shoulders; my face was narrow and rather lantern-jawed, with a big mouth, and English Channel grey eyes under very straight brows. My arms were toned – almost too toned, I had visible biceps. But when I took a step back I could see that all those lonely, obsessive hours in the gym had paid off in other ways. I had a shape which, in the right kind of clothes (the sort I never wore), would be described as hourglass.

Our relationship jerked forward in mono-syllables. Well, we had no need of words...

'When?' I asked him next time.

We were sitting up in bed with his arm round my shoulders.

'Whenever you like. What's to stop us?'

'Nothing,' I agreed. But something in my voice made him pull his head back to get a better look at me.

'What's up?'

'Nothing.'

'Changed your mind?'

'Of course not!'

'It's a woman's prerogative.'

'Well I haven't.'

He turned my face towards him. 'I know that look ... Something's bothering you.'

'All right,' I said. 'It's my parents.'

'They'll be over the moon, girl!'

'That's the trouble. I can't stand the

thought of all the fuss. It makes me feel sick. I can't handle it.'

'No fuss then. But you've got to tell them.'

'Afterwards,' I said firmly. 'We'll tell them afterwards.'

He shrugged, and squeezed my shoulders. 'If you say so. Won't they be hurt?'

'They'll be cool,' I said, which was a lie: the last thing they'd be was cool. And they might be hurt, a little. But a secret wedding would fit in with my role as resident rebel, and I was sure the surprise and pleasure would outweigh any sense of injury they might have about not being told earlier.

'In that case, I'll get the licence.'

'What about your Dad?'

'Same thing. If yours can wait, so can he.'

'Don't not tell him for my sake,' I said. 'I wouldn't mind.'

'He'll know soon enough.'

'You sure?'

'It wouldn't be right. You ought to meet him, though.'

'Whenever you like.'

I was surprised by what a big man Fergal's dad was. Somehow the mention of his impaired mobility had conjured up a picture of someone frail and stooped. But you could see where Fergal got it from; John Docherty was built on a grand scale. He moved slowly because of pain in his knees, and it was like having a great caber, or a pine with loosened roots, weaving about the place. Because I was with him Fergal didn't use his key, but rang the bell, and I noticed one of those fall-alarm buttons hanging on a hook in the hall – the old man must have taken it off before opening the door.

He also had the sort of perfect old-fashioned gentlemanly manners that bring out the lady in a person – even me – expressing genuine delight at meeting me, insisting I take the best armchair that was still warm from his backside, and creaking unsteadily out to the tiny kitchen to make tea. The flat, in a bland, council-built old people's complex, was homely and pin-neat, like his son's. On the mantelpiece was a photograph of Fergal's mother as a 1950s full-skirted bride, and one of the young Fergal in a shirt and tie, with no front teeth.

When he went to make tea, I half got up to go and help, but Fergal made a 'Leave him to it' gesture and said, 'Cheers, Dad.'

Over tea and biscuits he asked me about my work and I asked him about his flat and his photographs, addressing him as Mr Docherty rather than John until invited to do otherwise, which happened quite soon.

There were absolutely no hints or heavy cues that I could detect, he behaved impeccably, though I was pretty sure, looking at the gorgeous, beaming Jean Docherty in her white lace, that I was not his idea of an attractive woman.

Apparently I was wrong. Surely it wasn't just that gentlemanly politeness that prompted him to say, as we stood in the hall about to leave: 'Monica, it's been a pleasure. It does my old heart good to have a pretty girl in here.'

I thanked him for the compliment and the tea and added, truthfully, how much I'd enjoyed meeting him.

'Come again whenever you like.' He turned to Fergal and they exchanged a manly but affectionate handshake.

'Bye, son.'

'Bye, Dad, thanks. See you Tuesday.'

John placed his other hand over his son's for a second and gave it a squeeze. 'Bye.'

In the street outside, I said: 'He's lovely.'

'All right, isn't he? Glad you liked him.'

And I was glad it was left at that, no arch references to my having passed some kind of test, or cheering the old boy up. In the car, I found myself seeing my parents through Fergal's eyes and reflecting that they weren't bad either.

Fergal broke a thoughtful silence by asking: 'By the way – you for church?'

'No.'

'Registry office do?'

'Absolutely.'

'You don't want to be on top of Snowdon or anything?'

I laughed. 'No!'

'Only you're so fit...' He put out his hand and squeezed my thigh appreciatively. 'Nothing would surprise me.'

The date we finally settled on, the first one that fitted with his shifts and mine and allowed for a night away afterwards, was the day of Tara's eighteenth at Mendlesham Mill. We discussed what to do and made a plan, which he considered pretty audacious, but was prepared to go along with since this was my family we were talking about and he had no option: I knew them; he didn't.

'You are coming, aren't you?' asked my mother over the phone, the day the invitations arrived.

'Yes.'

'Oh good, that will be – sorry?' I heard Dad calling out in the background. 'Yes, yes...! Your father says not to let them keep you at work.'

'I won't.'

'She won't! Anyway, it'll be so nice to have all the family together. Do you remember Donald and Ann, from Cirencester? They're coming, possibly bringing the whole gang. Which reminds me I must make sure they let Rose know if they are, because it's a sit-down lunch and the Mill will need to know exact numbers.'

This reminded me of something, too, and I called my sister.

'Rosie?'

'Mon, hi – can you make it?'

She was so sweet, I did love her. 'Try and stop me. Rosie—'

'Do I hear a "but"?'

'Not at all. Rosie – I know this is a cheek, but can I bring Fergal?'

'Can you?' She gave such a shriek I had to move the receiver away from my ear. 'Too right you can!'

'Are you sure Tara won't mind?'

'Mind? It'll make her day.'

It was just as well she couldn't see my expression of agonized anxiety.

'I don't want a big fuss. It's Tara's do.'

'That's why I'm getting my fussing done now!' whooped Rose. 'Don't worry, Mon, you can rely on me.'

I knew I could. But this was one occasion when I had opted, even with Rosie, for the truth but not the whole truth. My biggest secret was going to stay that way for the time being. Our witnesses were going to be an old mate of Fergal's (not in the fire service) and whoever we could find hanging about on the day.

For almost the first time in my life I was excercised about what to wear. I knew that whatever I wore it wouldn't matter to Fergal, but I wanted to pay him the compliment of at least putting some thought into it. The safest option was an enhanced version of my usual look – a haircut, a new pair of trousers and some sort of flattering, non-aggressive top without writing on it. But the more I trawled the shops the more bored and discouraged I felt. Everything that I could afford, in the high-street chains, and even in the indoor fleamarket looked the same. I was sick of it all. Some sort of change would be fun, but it was so long since I'd considered such a thing that no ideas sprang to mind. Under normal circumstances I might have called Rosie and enlisted her help – her instincts in these matters were sound, and she knew me well enough not to let me look ridiculous. But I was determined to go it alone.

I was returning from A & E with Kidder, one of our girls who had OD'd a bit on the self-harming, when I spotted the sign by a garden gate, on the outskirts of one of the villages between us and the hospital. I must have driven past it dozens of times, but perhaps because I was sensitized to such things this was the first time I'd noticed it.

EXCHANGE AND SMART DRESS AGENCY
SURPRISE YOURSELF!

Okay, I said to myself. You're on.

The moment I came off my shift I drove the five miles or so back to Stoke Hetherington, only to find it was one of those posh hobby-businesses with idiosyncratic opening hours to suit the lady of the house. I nearly packed it in there and then, but decided that was pathetic, and went back again a couple of days later.

The sign said 'Ring and Enter', so I did.

Here's the funny thing. In spite of the bell the proprietor, obviously a trusting soul, didn't appear at once. I wandered all alone into the front room where the racks of clothes stood bathed in the afternoon sun that poured through the high sash window. And for only the second time in my life, I fell in love.

I was standing there slack-jawed with desire when the woman came in.

'Seen anything you like?'

I pointed.

'Ah yes...' She smiled in a comfortable, confident sort of way as she took the dress off the rail. 'Quite right.'

I don't know why she said that, because the dress was so not me, it was ridiculous. She just seemed to realize that this was a non-rational attraction. When I put it on the zip wouldn't go past my shoulder blades, but she pointed out that the previous owner, for whom it had been made, had included a bag of offcuts from the original pattern.

'I can't sew a stitch!' I moaned, heaving at the sides.

'Don't worry,' she said soothingly. 'I know a woman who can. She does a lot of alterations.'

'That'll cost.'

'I'm sure we can reach an accommodation.'

It was as though I were involved in some gentle conspiracy, as if this wise woman had put a spell on me. If so, it worked. I bought the dress – even secondhand it was the most expensive thing I was ever going to buy – and arranged to collect it in a week.

'WOW!'

That was the best of our monosyllables so

far. Until Fergal I'd never had that effect on anyone, but this time I could tell he was speaking for everyone in the room, and they were a mixed bunch: his old school mate, the registrar, and the young couple who'd been registering the birth of their baby.

Fergal dragged his eyes away from me and looked at the registrar: 'Am I allowed to kiss her first?'

The registrar smiled. 'Be my guest.'

And now Fergal and I were Mr and Mrs Docherty, arriving a little late at Tara's lunch party at Mendlesham Mill. We didn't so much as hold hands, but marched in side by side, heads up and shoulders swinging, like a couple of storm troopers, pumping iron, fired up with love and the extraordinary thing that we'd done.

The girl on the desk pointed us in the right direction, I could feel her eyes on me. That covert, admiring look from another woman was the final proof that every penny I'd spent was worth it.

Fergal pushed open the door of the beautiful, old, timbered room where my nearest and dearest were drinking champagne. My lovely niece Tara was on the far side and her face, when she saw us, was a study. And in the mirror behind her I could see what she saw, and it was a terrific, mind-blowing, humbling moment.

There was Monica – stroppy, stocky, sideways Monica – in black biker's boots and a dress of sprayed-on satin in fire-engine red, and next to her, the sexiest man in the room.

And do you know? Even though it was her day, Tara ran towards me and threw her arms round my neck. And everyone cheered.

Pauline

In the supermarket, you were being manipulated from the moment you walked in. No, Pauline reminded herself, from before you walked in. Even the outside of the building was constructed in such a way as to make you feel you were doing something sociable, respectable, even, instead of colluding in what most intelligent people who watched television now knew was a pretty ruthless commercial operation. The building was low rise and gabled, with friendly, domestic-looking pitched roofs, more like a ranch, a travel lodge or a big friendly bungalow than the most successful retail operation in Britain.

But once inside the big friendly bungalow, you were on another planet – Planet Shopping – and normal rules didn't apply. The temperature was strictly controlled, kept at blood temperature so you scarcely knew where you ended and the air began; there was white noise, to lull you into a zombie-like state; over the white noise, at regular intervals, little ding-dong messages were played about special offers – 3 for 2s, WIGIGS, and bonus points – but at a discreet, non-intrusive level, so you had to concentrate to catch them; nearest the door were the flowers, banks of them, to give the place the air of a market, and beyond them the bakery, giving off an appetising smell, and the fruit and veg – all the fresh stuff, to make you feel good about yourself even if all you were coming in for was a pork pie and a can of coke; the aisles were patrolled by senior staff in blazers, whose lapel badges proclaimed that they were there to help, and the check-out girls asked how you were today and whether you needed any help packing, even if you only had half a dozen items; the messages on the public address system always ended with a polite and appreciative 'thank you', unless they were for members of staff in which case they had a crispness that inspired confidence – the inhabitants of Planet Shopping had every-thing under control, the visitors had nothing to fear, and nothing to do but relax and make their purchases, which would cost almost nothing; and if you wanted, it didn't have to stop there – by the check-out, along with the sweets, the environmentally friend-ly carriers, the recipe cards and the store's lifestyle magazine were all the brightly coloured leaflets that told you how to buy that lifestyle; the mortgage, the insurance, the internet provider, the mobile phone network, the car, the holidays, the health plan.

In other words, for next to nothing, you could yourself become a resident of Planet Shopping and not have a care in the world.

Pauline was fully aware of all of this, so when she went to the out of town superstore, it was with her eyes open and her brain engaged. She was not manipulated as others were because she knew the score. She made a running list during the week and stuck to it. She took a positive pride in stalking past the temptingly placed discounted wine (stacked in boxes to give the impression of careless Mediterranean abundance), and the nice women peddling bite-size chunks of cheese on cocktail sticks. Pauline knew what was going on and was above it, beyond its reach. If they repositioned a product she wanted, in order to run her past the temptation of a thousand others, she sought it out and not a single impulse-buy went into the basket. Pauline was not to be pushed around. The superstore didn't manipulate her, she used it.

As for her conscience, that was clear too.

Once a week, on a Saturday, she and Roger went to the farmers' market on the other side of town and bought locally grown produce and eggs that were so fresh you quite often found a small feather in the carton. The supermarket was a convenience which young working professionals would be downright foolish – not to mention extravagant – to ignore, but you owed it to yourself, the farmers, the poorer countries and the environment, to be an ethical consumer where possible.

Pauline was twenty-nine – or in her thirtieth year as she preferred to think of it. She looked forward to being thirty, which she saw not so much in terms of *Friends*, or even *Bridget Jones*, but of officially ending one's youth and getting on with the business of being grown-up. At thirty, one was no longer a girl, but a woman – something Pauline had felt for ages.

She and Roger were not yet married, but they planned to tie the knot in two years' time, when they were well established. Even now they were better established than most couples. They had a small house with a huge mortgage in the whimsically-named Balzac Road. It was a new house – well, relatively new, the estate had been built in the late seventies during the town council's brief surge of European feeling, and all the roads were named after famous Europeans. Pauline, though she had never read any Balzac, counted herself lucky not to be in Garibaldi Buildings or Robespierre Court which, as you might expect, were positive nests of delinquency.

The house in Balzac Road was their second property together. When they'd met Pauline had been renting a nice little flat over the dry cleaners in the high street, and Roger had still been living at home. She liked to cook, and he was soon having supper at Pauline's several times a week. It was soon pretty clear they were meant for each other and the obvious next step was to get on the first rung of the ladder, which was another flat – bigger but not quite so well-appointed – in a small block on the site of the old post office. Roger wasn't all that handy to begin with, but he was a quick learner and after three years the equity in this flat was such that they could begin looking for a house.

Balzac Road had one double bedroom and two rooms for midgets; a double-aspect lounge/dining room (one of its biggest selling points and the reason Pauline had gone for it) and a galley kitchen which, once Roger had removed the tiles with laughing pigs on, was perfectly acceptable. The bathroom – low-level suite included, but you couldn't have everything – had been pink and beige with random entwined sea-horses, but once it was aquamarine it was improved beyond all measure. At the front there was a strip of grass which ran along the whole terrace, but each house had a stepping-stone path to its front door. At the back, Roger built a patio and the rest of the area was laid to grass. They had tubs and baskets for a splash of colour in the summer.

Pauline was senior receptionist at an opticians in the high street. Roger was a sales executive at the Japanese car franchise on the ring road, where he had twice won the salesman of the year award. Pauline hoped that before too long Roger would be able to use his sales and administration skills to get himself a more prestigious job and then in the fullness of time, his own business. He wasn't as ambitious as her but then he wouldn't be the one having the baby, when that came along.

They were a devoted couple, and they wanted the same things – a secure, happy, comfortable life, uneventful in the best possible way. Neither of them ever had cause to doubt the other, there was no jealousy in their partnership, which was a calm one, based on shared values.

Not that Pauline was complacent. A relationship had to be worked at, and even in this day and age a woman had a duty to look after her man. She prided herself on her appearance, looked after all their finances, cooked a new dish at least once a month, and never had a headache. Though this last area, it had to be said, was the one in which she and Roger might be said to be least successful. Not that they didn't do it once or twice a week which she knew from her reading and from listening to friends in a similar situation (she was discreet herself) was above average; and they were reasonably experimental as well, Pauline knew the dangers of getting stuck in a rut. But the truth was that Pauline had never had an orgasm. Or not with Roger. She knew this because from time to time she had succeeded in giving herself one and the intense pleasure and loss of control had been almost frightening. On each occasion the guilt had shadowed her for days like a slinking, grubby grey dog she was sure everyone else must be able to see.

She never mentioned this of course. That would have been unthinkable, far too embarrassing and besides it would have been insulting to Roger, implying that he was doing something wrong, or not enough, or that she didn't care for him, none of which was true.

Her rationale – and Pauline was nothing if not rational – was that sex was simply not the most important thing in a long-term relationship. Love, companionship, shared interests and goals, a matching sense of humour: these were the things that formed the bedrock of a couple's happiness, the things that would bind them together and carry them through the years. Physical attraction might be the reason for two people first getting together, but it was only natural that its effects would fade somewhat with time, as other factors took over.

There was only one problem with this rationale, which was that overwhelming physical attraction had not been the main reason she and Roger had started going out. Admittedly Roger was good-looking and well-presented and she liked that in a man, and he had told her since that her smartness (in both senses) was something that appealed to him; but their gravitating towards one another had been more due to their mutual recognition of a kindred spirit. So in a very real sense, Pauline told herself, they were soul-mates, which surely far outweighed the sex thing ... But she was alive to the dangers of complacency and kept her eye on things.

Because of her commitment to ethical shopping and local produce, Pauline's supermarket shop consisted of dry goods and basics – toilet paper, toiletries, cleaning materials, tins and bottles. She and Roger weren't great drinkers but they took an interest in wine and were educating themselves, and Roger liked a beer at weekends while he was doing jobs around the house.

In the pet-food aisle (Pauline and Roger didn't have pets, but she was heading towards detergents) she bumped into Kelly, who worked at the supermarket. Pauline and Kelly had been at school together, but since then Kelly's life had not followed the same steady upward curve. She'd done poorly in her GCSEs, was equally unsuccessful in retakes at the local FE college and since then had concentrated on waiting at tables, pulling pints, stacking shelves and, as she put it, Having a Good Time. Pauline could think of nothing worse than the round of pubbing, clubbing, boozing and shagging that Kelly so enjoyed, and she suspected (though without any malice) that Kelly might also constitute the good time had by all.

In spite of the disparity in their circumstances, Kelly was always friendly.

'Hi Pauline, how you doing?'

'Cheers Kelly, fine thanks.'

'How's Rog?'

'He's really well.'

Kelly gazed at her, beaming. For some reason both the gaze and the broad smile made Pauline uncomfortable. They were like a searchlight, exposing her. She sensed that even though Kelly earned almost nothing and was still living at home with her mother and her mother's boyfriend, she would not want to swap lives. Which was fine, because Pauline wouldn't either.

'Doing a big shop as usual,' said Kelly.

'Yes. Like to get the dull stuff out of the way.'

'As you do.'

They stood smiling at one another, and then Pauline said, 'Oh well...' and began to move away.

'Hang on,' said Kelly, 'I'm glad I saw you. I'm having a get-together for my thirtieth on Saturday week, you and Rog want to come?'

So Kelly had reached the magic three-oh before her! Pauline could scarcely believe it, and her momentary confusion prevented her from coming up with a quick excuse.

'Thanks, a party – lovely.'

'Rockefella's, eight o'clock,' said Kelly. 'Don't be late or I'll be wasted.'

'I'll check.'

'No need to let me know,' said Kelly. 'It's a free for all, just turn up.'

'Why not?' said Roger. 'Might be a laugh.'

'It'll be horrendous,' said Pauline. 'You know it will. Kelly as good as told me she'd be completely drunk all evening.'

Roger considered this. He liked Kelly, what he'd seen of her, and he and Pauline had both been working hard both in the office and at home, it would do them good to go out and party.

'It's her thirtieth,' he pointed out. 'A girl's entitled to have a drink on her thirtieth.'

'Have a drink, yes, but not—'

Roger put his arms round Pauline and snuggled up to her. 'It's nice of her to ask us, let's go.'

In the end Pauline acquiesced, though not with a very good grace. Later, when they were going to bed, she put her arms round his neck and apologized.

'What for?'

'Sorry I was grumpy about Kelly's do.'

'You weren't. You're not keen, but it'll be okay – you'll be with me.'

It was a joke of sorts, but she didn't smile.

'We don't have to stay late.'

'Course we don't. And Kelly'll be pleased.'

'Yes,' she said, but she still looked worried.

Roger had noticed this in his partner – an inability or, no, an unwillingness, to let go and enjoy herself. It was as though like a shark if she stopped moving, she would perish. He loved and admired her more than she knew – more, he acknowledged in his heart of hearts, than she loved and admired him – but he wished she were happier. She was reasonably content, but contentment, for her, consisted in ticking boxes, maintaining objectives, achieving goals and replacing them with others.

The inability to let go extended into other areas of their shared life. Roger knew their lovemaking left her unsatisfied, but she would have been appalled to know that he knew, so he never mentioned it. He was ashamed of his craven collusion, but what could he do? The moment to say something, if there had ever been one, was long past, and their mutual denial was set in stone. They still had regular sex, but sometimes he thought it would be better if they didn't. The absence of a sex life would have been a real, obvious problem, a sign that things weren't good between them, and maybe they'd have talked about it. As things were they were living a pretence, which he found deeply dispiriting.

Surprisingly, it didn't seem to bother Pauline. Roger accepted what he'd heard anecdotally, that these things were different for women. Most of his mates were still single and their view was that even the girls who put out were doing it for some reason other than lust. Roger's grandfather had once said in his hearing that while men put up with the love to get the sex, women put up with the sex to get the love. That had sounded pretty old-fashioned even then, but there might be some truth in it. He believed, and Jesus! how he hoped, that Pauline loved him, because he adored her. He just didn't seem able to bring her – the very word was embarrassing – joy.

Ironically, Pauline's full-on busyness and energy, her attention to detail, were part of what he found sexy in her. A whiff of starch in a woman was a well-known turn-on. She always looked terrific. She looked every bit as good on a winter's night after a bath, in her big dressing gown and fluffy slippers, with her hair in a towel, as she did when she was all dressed up for a do. She took care of herself, she was always clean, her skin smelt sweet and her hair – mmm ... Just thinking

128

of it made him close his eyes with remembered pleasure. And she took trouble, too, over the things that didn't show: she wore pretty underwear, and if he ever bought her anything along those lines she'd wear that, too. And yet ... Roger couldn't help but sense that all these things were, for her, part of the job of being his girlfriend; a job which like every other one she undertook, she did conscientiously and to the best of her ability. He knew he was lucky to have such a woman, when there were plenty – probably these days the majority – who were out for number one and wanted laughs, money, attention and sexual satisfaction and would kick a bloke into touch without a second thought if he didn't come up with the goods. Ladettes, bitches, bikes, ballbreakers – Pauline was so not one of those. But it would have been easier for both of them if she'd paid more attention to the real stuff – the stuff under the surface.

It was odd that Roger should have dwelt so much on all this because he was not, by nature or upbringing, introspective. He was a tall, handsome young man whom people instinctively liked and trusted, and this meant he'd had an easy ride through life so far. He wasn't fantastically clever or gifted in any particular direction, but he could turn his hand to things. At the showroom they thought the world of him, because he didn't fit into the usual mould of car salesmen. He was quieter, gentler – especially with the female customers – knowledgeable without being a smart arse. With Roger, the sales seemed effortless; the car sold itself, which was the idea really. The numbers spoke for themselves; but he didn't come over as pushy, and that meant he was popular. The other blokes knew he was in a steady relationship with a mortgage, and he got teased about that, but not unkindly.

Most of them had met Pauline once or twice, at work-related events – the Christmas bash, the top salesmen's trip to Paris – and Roger had been proud of the impression she'd made on his colleagues. Because the two of them had been together so long, and bought a house, the guys probably pictured a rather dull, mousy person. But Pauline was pretty with a great figure, confident and elegant, the sort of woman it was good to have on your arm when you walked in. They might not want Roger's level of commitment, but they could see he'd done well for himself.

The only bloke from Drayton Daewoo that Roger saw outside work was Bob, who ran the Servicing Department. Being a department manager he was a bit older than the others, and married, so Roger felt they had something in common.

They went for a drink after work not long after the exchange about Kelly's birthday party.

'How's that lovely lady of yours?' asked Bob.

'She's good. Working hard.'

'Like you.'

'That's right.'

'You get to play as well, I hope.'

'We do,' replied Roger, and was pleased to be able to add: 'We're off to a big thirtieth at the end of the month.'

'Where at?'

'Rockefella's, in town.'

'Heard of it. Can't say I know it.'

Roger back-pedalled a bit. 'It's not all that. Fancy beers and cocktails, bit of a rip-off joint. Music's all right though, should be a good night.'

'Dancing?'

'Yeah, bit of that.'

Bob shook his head. 'Good luck to you mate. I've got two left feet. Sheila's stopped trying to get me out on the floor, why embarrass the two of us? Fortunately the girls are happy to boogie on their own and I enjoy watching.'

'Pauline's a good dancer,' said Roger.

'I'll bet. What about you?'

'I'm no Travolta. Couple of drinks and I don't mind. Give it a go.'

'Brave man.'

This conversation stuck in Roger's memory, probably because it had conjured up a picture of the party. He found himself wondering what Pauline would wear. She tended to buy good things, fairly plain, and look after them. You wouldn't catch Pauline in a sequinned denim mini and a boob-tube. Classy classics were more her line. He sometimes thought she could afford to be a little more daring, show off a bit. Not that he wanted her to look tarty, he couldn't stand that, but she was so great-looking she could afford to flaunt it. She had a nice black shift dress that she wore with pearl earrings and black pumps, but he hoped she wouldn't go that route for Kelly's event. A small part of Roger wanted her to outshine the other girls on this one occasion, to strut her stuff and show what she was made of.

He made tentative enquiries.

'What you going to wear on Saturday?' he asked. 'To Kelly's?'

'My black, probably.'

'Always nice,' he agreed. 'You always look good in that.'

'I know I wear it a lot,' said Pauline, 'but at least on this occasion I won't blend into the background.'

'How do you mean?'

'Well if I know anything about it they'll all be in glitter tops and pvc trousers.'

'What about the women?' asked Roger.

This didn't get a laugh. 'My black will really stand out.'

'Right.'

They went on watching *Wife Swap* for a bit, and during the commercial break, Roger said: 'You know you ought to go for a bit of flash for a change. You'd look amazing.'

'You're fed up with the black?'

'You're joking, no – it's classic. But you could knock their socks off, Paul.'

He sensed a slight prickle. 'What do you suggest?'

'Oh, I don't know...' He laughed. 'Strapless, frontless, backless gold lamé?'

Because he'd made it obvious he was joking, she laughed too. 'That'd clear the floor.'

'Whatever.' He put his arm round her. 'You always look triffic.'

Joking or not, Pauline found herself reflecting on this conversation. It was the case –

anecdotally, as she understood it – that most men in serious relationships wanted their partners to cover up in public. Plunging necklines, buttock-skimming hems, keyhole apertures, bare midriffs, all kinds of daring exposure, were considered 'tarty'. Why, went the argument, should the whole world have the opportunity to ogle a chap's goods? And yet here was Roger actually suggesting she flash more flesh ... The suggestion deserved careful consideration.

She decided to bounce it off Trudy, her friend at work. Trudy was a little younger than Pauline, but engaged, with a ring on her finger and a wedding at the Garden House planned for the summer after next.

When the opticians closed at the end of the afternoon, and they were tidying up the reception area, Pauline asked casually: 'Trudy, what sort of thing does Sean like you in?'

'What? How do you mean?'

'What does he like you to wear?'

'Thong and a push-up bra – no, he doesn't mind. I wear what I like.'

'Really? He doesn't ever – suggest things?'

'Pauline...' Trudy pulled a cheeky face. 'Have you been in that traffic warden's outfit again?'

'No, no, not that sort of thing. Just generally.'

Trudy saw this was to be a serious conversation, and shook her head. 'No. Let's be honest, blokes don't care, do they? They don't even notice half the time. Let's face it, on our big day, if Sean remembers I wore white and didn't have spinach on my teeth it'll be a result.'

'I see,' said Pauline.

Trudy put her head on one side. 'Why do you ask?'

'We're going to a friend's thirtieth. I get the impression Roger'd like me to go a bit more flash than usual.'

'No kidding?' Trudy leaned her hip on the desk and folded her arms. 'Good sign.'

'How do you work that out?'

'Shows he's interested. Shows he cares. He loves you, babe.'

Pauline shuffled papers to conceal her blushes. Trudy was so forthright.

'And?' asked Trudy.

'I can't make up my mind. I don't do flash, as a rule. It doesn't suit me.'

'You've got the figure for it.'

'It's more a question of – I don't know – personality.'

Trudy shrugged. 'If you've got it, flaunt it. Give Roger a treat.'

Put like that, Pauline could see that it was, if not her duty exactly, at least a good idea to go along with the suggestion.

'Hey!' Roger zapped the telly and gave Pauline his full attention. 'Get you!'

'Do you like it?'

'Do I! Paul, girl, you look bloody lovely.'

'Thanks.' She made a little frowning, uncertain face, and looked down at herself. 'Are you sure?'

'Sure?' Roger got up and stood in front of her, putting his hands on her bare shoulders and running them down the warm, slippery curves of her body. 'You're gorgeous. There won't be anyone there to touch you.'

'I feel very strange.'

'Is that right...?' He bent and dropped a kiss on the smooth, scented curve of her neck. 'It doesn't show. Oh, Paul...'

'Roger, darling.' She sensed his arousal and stiffened. 'Not now.'

'Later, then. I want you to keep the dress on when we get home.'

'All right.'

He slid his hands down her back and cupped her bottom, which felt taut under the thick satin. 'Paul...'

'What?'

'Do me a favour?'

'It depends.'

'Go commando.'

She pulled back. 'What?'

'You know what they say: red dress and no knickers.'

'And you know what they mean: common.'

He laughed, partly to bring himself down, dampen his desire. 'I just thought it would be sexy. No one would know but me. It could be our secret.'

'I couldn't,' she said. 'Let's go. Have you locked up at the back?'

It was a twenty-minute drive to Rockefella's, in the centre of town. By coincidence, they had Simply Red on the music centre, but Roger knew better than to comment. The transformation was so incredible, he didn't want to push his luck.

Once they'd parked, and were about to get out, Pauline said: 'By the way, I did it.'

For a moment he wasn't sure what she was on about. 'You did?'

'I took them off.'

He could scarcely believe his ears. Incredulously he put out his hand.

'No.' She pushed it gently away. 'You'll have to take my word for it.'

As he locked the car door, she began walking across the car park, a few paces ahead of him. And he could see she'd been telling the truth.

Inside, the club was absolutely rammed. The doorman gave them a token for one cocktail each on the house, courtesy of Kelly. They fought their way to the bar. The DJ was Sly Fox, well known locally for getting everyone going. While Roger got them in, Pauline looked around and finally spotted Kelly who was dancing with no one in particular and everyone in general, waving her arms above her head and tossing her streaked mane from side to side like a maddened palomino pony. She was wearing a silver halter-top with no bra, and her breasts were bouncing about like a couple of rabbits trying to get out of a sack.

As the track ended and Sly blended into the next one, Kelly spotted them and jumped up and down, arms in the air, mouthing, 'Come on!'

Roger put his lips to Pauline's ear. 'Want to dance?'

She turned so he could lip read. 'Drink first!'

'Sure!'

He'd got himself a Coltrayne's, so both the cocktails (Pleasure Seekers – vodka, Grand

Marnier and passion fruit juice) were for Pauline.

It was hot in here and she drank the first one quite fast. But she was glad of the crush because it made her feel a little less conspicuous. At least the dress was classy – no label, so probably dressmaker-made – and fitted like a glove, but there was no denying that it was a statement, and one she didn't usually make. She had never felt so conspicuous in her life.

'Whaaa-hey!' With Kelly there was no need to lip-read, she was well into party mode and could have made herself heard over a nuclear explosion.

'Hi Kelly. Happy birthday!'

'You look HOT!' Kelly embraced Pauline. She had teamed the silver top with black lycra hot-pants, a silver chain belt, and black and silver platform high heels with a buckled ankle-strap.

'So do you!'

'Rog, you better watch out!' yelled Kelly, flinging her arms round his neck. 'She's HOT!'

Obligingly, Roger returned the embrace, giving Kelly's bare back a pat and bawling: 'I know!'

'Come and dance!'

'We were just—' began Roger, but Kelly

had grabbed Pauline by the wrist and Pauline only just had time to put her Pleasure Seeker down on the bar before she was being dragged through the melee into the thick of things.

Roger could no longer see her, but he could imagine her, doing her special little dance step, side to side with her forearms held out like half-open wings. He was pleased in a way that Kelly had broken the ice and hauled her off. There'd be plenty of time for him to dance with her later, when she was all loosened up and sweating a bit ... Somewhere on the floor of Rockefella's, if memory served, there was an area of mirror tiles, he did hope Pauline wasn't dancing just there. To dispel this worrying thought he ordered himself another Coltrayne's, and pulled the spare Pleasure Seeker towards him protectively.

Pauline was quite happy dancing with the girls, several of whom she knew. Kelly was behaving like her agent, or a fairground barker, shouting out to anyone who'd listen: 'Meet my hot friend ... Surprised she can move at all ... Wicked frock or what?' Not that it was necessary, because it was pretty obvious she, Pauline, was being admired. She admitted cautiously to herself that the dress was a success, and began to move more freely, swaying her hips and rippling her arms, enjoying herself. Kelly was a tactile sort of person, and every few minutes she'd hurl herself on Pauline and clasp her to her unfettered bosom, pushing her pelvis into hers and gyrating suggestively, to loud applause.

'Let's give them something to talk about!'

Pauline wasn't comfortable with that, and after the third time she disentangled herself and shouted that she needed another drink.

'Make sure you come back!' yelled Kelly. 'Or I'll come and fetch you.'

Pauline reached the bar, gasping for air. Roger's half-full Coltrayne's and her second cocktail stood side by side, but there was no sign of Roger.

One of the barman saw her looking round and said cheekily in her ear:

'Gone to the little boys' room, darling, anything I can do?'

'No, thank you.'

'You're my fantasy, know that? Lady in Red...' he warbled, and she had to smile.

She picked up her glass and took a sip. Like all cocktails it was delicious – sweet and heady. Across the other side she saw Roger come back in, but almost at once a couple of guys hailed him, and there was a lot of arm-punching and shoulder-squeez-ing, one of them stuffed a bottle in his hand.

She looked away, and as she did so she couldn't help feel someone watching her, further along the bar. Pauline's gaze flicked over the person, only long enough to register that it was a woman, with dark hair and dark clothes. Pauline had the awful feeling that maybe it was someone she knew from another place, another context – per-haps one of the optician's customers – looking at her in astonished disapproval. She did hope not. In the other direction she was conscious of Kelly summoning her again. She wasn't quite ready for that, so she headed off, making her way around the side of the room to the Chill-Out Lounge.

In here it was dark, with pink uplighters and velvet sofas and banquettes. You could still hear the thud of the disco, but there was some panpipe music playing to create a more tranquil mood. This early in the evening there were only two couples snog-ging, and another deep in some sort of intense exchange, the young man talking insistently in a low voice and the girl crying. Pauline wasn't too worried, it was a fairly standard scenario.

She sat down in a corner with her cocktail. With her free hand she smoothed the dress over her thighs, then anxiously tweaked the edge of the strapless bodice to make sure she wasn't about to burst forth.

'Don't change a thing.'

The voice came from Pauline's left, in the other corner of the banquette, and it took her by surprise, she hadn't known there was anyone there.

'I'm sorry?'

'You look glorious.'

Glorious? Pauline peered. Her eyes were not yet accustomed to the gloom, but she could make out a pale face and a hand. As she looked, a thin whisp of smoke appeared, hovered and evaporated.

'You don't mind compliments from a stranger, do you?'

'I don't think I've ever had any.'

She could see now that the other person was a woman – the woman, in fact, who had been watching her at the bar. She'd been some distance away, and the dance floor was packed; how had she got in here so quickly? She must have followed her.

In spite of the 'stranger' reference, Pauline asked warily: 'We don't know each other, do we?'

The woman made a sniffing sound, which Pauline recognized as a laugh. 'I think I should have remembered.'

'I don't always dress like this. In fact I never dress like this.'

'In that case I consider myself extremely fortunate to be here tonight.'

The woman leaned forward to stub out her cigarette, and Pauline saw a pale face with high, wide cheekbones, a square jaw, straight black eyebrows and lashes that cast a shadow. When the woman glanced up, the impact of her eyes made Pauline blink.

'Now I've finished that horrid thing,' said the woman, 'may I?'

'Oh, yes, of course. Do.'

The woman moved closer to Pauline on the banquette. She wore a black roll-neck sweater and black trousers. Her wavy dark hair was brushed uncompromisingly straight back, but because it was thick and wiry it stood out, like a frame, around her face. She brought with her a glass of water, with ice, but sat with folded arms, staring at Pauline.

'You are without doubt the best thing I've seen all week.'

'Thank you,' said Pauline. At last her good manners came to the rescue. 'How do you know Kelly?'

'Kelly?'

'It's her birthday.'

'Then many happy returns to her, whoever she may be.'

'You don't know her?'

The woman shook her head. 'But you do, I take it.'

'We were at school together.'

'How long ago?'

'Oh – fifteen years...?'

'M-hmm.'

There followed a silence, during which the pan pipes played their cool, watery, mysterious music, and the woman stared smiling at Pauline. There was something strange in the atmosphere – a charge which emanated from the woman. What with her black clothes and her severe, striking appearance, it was not hard to imagine she might be casting a spell, and Pauline moved quickly to deflect it, holding out her hand and saying: 'I'm Pauline Frear, by the way.'

'Jane.' The woman placed her hand in Pauline's and removed it again, as if it were a key. 'Nice to meet you, Pauline.'

'Sorry, I didn't catch—'

'No, you didn't. Just Jane.'

There was another silence, awkward on Pauline's part, composed and thoughtful on Jane's.

'Do you—' began Pauline and then, realizing she had been about to say 'come here often', hesitated and changed it to 'often come here?'

'From time to time, just to watch. It's not my sort of place.'

'Nor me.'

'Really? You surprise me.'

'I'm not the clubbing sort. Roger and I—'

'Ah, Roger. Tell me about him.'

Why on earth should I? thought Pauline. But that didn't stop her going ahead.

'He's my boyfriend. He's here with me as a matter of fact.'

'I believe I saw him earlier.' Jane glanced around. 'Where is he now?'

'Talking to some friends. I needed a break.'

'From the birthday party?'

'Yes.'

Jane glanced at her watch, a man's watch on a broad, black strap. 'The night is young, and already you need a break?'

'I can only do this sort of thing in short bursts.'

Jane smiled and gave her little sniffing laugh. 'And Roger?'

'He's happy wherever he is. Easy-going – you know.'

'Yes,' said Jane, 'I know.'

Oddly, Pauline felt that she did.

Roger was tied up with Ian and Bobbo for

longer than he intended. He hadn't seen either of them in years and they had some serious catching up to do.

'Still single, mate?' asked Bobbo. 'Still out there?'

'No, I'm with Pauline – remember Pauline?'

'Can't say I do.' Bobbo looked at Ian, who shook his head. 'Give us a clue.'

'See for yourself,' said Roger. 'She's over at the bar. The one in red.'

He was prickling with excitement, but it drained away when, in spite of craning and jumping up and down, they couldn't see her.

'Looks like she found a better offer,' Ian said, then added amiably, 'Only joking. Gone for a pee I expect.'

'Or out there.' Roger nodded in the direction of the seething sea of dancers. 'Celebrating with Kelly.'

'That Kelly...' Bobbo shook his head happily. 'Some things never change.'

'Thank Christ,' said Ian. 'I wouldn't push her out.'

'You'd have to, mate, she'd never go of her own accord!'

Roger laughed with them. Kelly had always been known as a girl who'd put out for any halfway decent bloke, but she was well-liked anyway. He only wished Pauline would reappear so he could show her off, demonstrate to these two old friends just how well he'd done for himself. He kept peering at the scrum on the dance floor, hoping for a flash of red, but it didn't happen.

After another Coltrayne's with the lads – at this rate he was going to have to call a taxi at the end of the evening – he headed back to the bar. Pauline's cocktail was gone, but that wasn't surprising, it could have chugged down anyone's neck. Suddenly, out of nowhere, Kelly was upon him.

'Rog! Aren't you going to dance with me on my birthday?'

She didn't wait for his answer but hauled him on to the floor. Out there in the middle it was Kellysville – all her mates, singing along and getting on down, and when he appeared an enormous cheer went up and he found himself the centre of more female attention than he'd had in years, his jacket pulled off, his belt undone, his hair ruffled and his cock squeezed by dozens of French-manicured hands. It wasn't unpleasant, but he could see where it was heading.

'I need to look for Pauline!' he yelled, hanging on to his trousers with one hand and fending off an enthusiastic redhead with the other.

'Forget it, mate!' bellowed Kelly, turning and rotating her backside against his. 'She could be anywhere! And you're with me now!'

'Oh well,' said Pauline. 'Time I went back in, I suppose.'

'If you must.' Jane took cigarettes and matches from her pocket and lit up. 'Do you really want to?'

'Well, it's Kelly's birthday—'

'So you said.' Jane looked at her, eyes narrowed, through the smoke. 'Do you think she's missing you?'

'Probably not, but—'

'Make that definitely. And where—' Jane glanced round pointedly – 'is Roger?'

'Still talking to—'

'So you see,' said Jane, 'you might as well stay here and talk to me.'

It was the sudden realization of how much she wanted to do exactly that, which made Pauline get to her feet.

'I'd love to, but duty calls.'

Another sniff. 'Duty ... Bless you.'

'Goodbye, it was nice meeting you.'

Jane smiled as if she heard something beyond the formulaic words.

'It's Jane Rowe, by the way.'

'Bye, Jane.'

Having now said goodbye twice, Pauline left the Chill-Out Lounge, with its soothing pinkish twilight, cool panpipes and soft velvet, and the unsettling still, dark presence of Jane Rowe, and went back to the party.

The floor was if anything even more crowded than before, but she spotted Roger instantly. It would have been hard not to, since he was the centre of attention, dancing like a dervish in his boxers, with a purple feather boa around his neck, the focal point of an admiring and vociferous crowd. He didn't see her, but Kelly did, and leapt in the air, beckoned her, as it were, with her whole body. Pauline ignored her and turned away, heading for the exit. Her face must have been white, because the doorman pushed the door open for her.

'Breath of fresh air, madam?'

She ignored that, too, but then something occurred to her and she turned back.

'Excuse me—'

'Yes?'

'I thought you ought to know – there's a man in there taking his clothes off on the dance floor.'

'Is that right?' The doorman's eyes lit up at the prospect of some actual bouncing.

'It may not be his fault, totally,' said Pauline. 'He's being sort of mobbed.'

'Birthday girls,' agreed the man, 'tell me about it.'

'But don't you have rules about that sort of thing?'

'We certainly do, madam. It isn't nice for the other customers. Thanks for telling me, I'll go and sort it out.' He gave her a frankly admiring glance. 'Hope the silliness didn't spoil your evening.'

'No,' said Pauline, 'I was leaving anyway.'

She went out into the street and down through the precinct into the carpark. She felt extremely conspicuous in her dress, and was glad when she reached the car. Her plan had been simply to drive away, but now two things prevented her. One was that although she felt stone-cold sober (in fact peculiarly calm considering Roger's antics) she remembered she'd had two cocktails and would be well over the limit. The other was that she had left her little evening bag, with her keys, somewhere in the club. This was a real worry, and she began to totter back as quickly as she could in her strappy sandals, her eyes smarting with tears.

There was a different, younger, doorman there when she got back – presumably his colleague was away dealing with Roger –

and he stood back for her with a flourish.

'Did anyone—?' she began, but then she saw Jane Rowe, standing in the lobby, holding out her bag.

'Yours, I think?'

'Yes!' Pauline took it and clasped it to her breast. If there was one thing she hated it was losing things. Quite apart from the inconvenience and upset, you felt such a fool.

'Thank you so much,' she said.

'My pleasure. It must have been an awful moment.'

'I am so, so grateful!' said Pauline. She and Jane were staring at each other during this exchange, she badly wanted to say something else, but wasn't quite sure what.

'Anyway,' said Jane, 'I was going to leave it with the management, but I'm glad I caught you.'

'Yes!'

The door to the club opened, and Jane glanced round.

'And here,' she said, 'unless I'm much mistaken, is Roger.'

Roger was dressed, but still buttoning his shirt and looked hot and unhappy. The older doorman was walking a little way behind with an indulgent half-smile on his face, making it clear he was not throwing

Roger out, merely returning to his post.

'Let's go,' said Pauline to Roger.

'Paul—'

'It doesn't matter. Let's just go.'

'I'll have to call a cab.'

The doorman said, 'I'll do that for you, sir.'

'I'm quite—' began Roger, but the doorman was already on his mobile.

'Be here in two ticks, rank's round the corner.'

'Thanks.'

Pauline looked round for Jane Rowe, but she'd gone. She felt suddenly devastated – tired, flat, disappointed; none of it to do with Roger for whom, now she'd calmed down, she felt merely sorry.

'Let's wait outside,' she said.

The taxi arrived almost at once, and they weren't going to talk in front of the driver, but to show Roger she bore no ill will, Pauline patted his knee. He gave her an agonized look in return.

The moment the front door closed behind them, he burst out: 'It wasn't my fault!'

'I know.'

'Kelly was dead set on making an idiot of me.'

'I could see that.'

'They ganged up on me.'

'I know.'

During this exchange, Pauline had moved past Roger into the kitchen, and was putting the kettle on. 'Tea?'

'I'm so sorry, Paul. It was so fucking embarrassing, and there was you looking like that, you didn't deserve—'

'Roger.' She placed her hand on his chest. 'Forget it. It's okay, honestly.'

He frowned anxiously and covered her hand with his, but she slipped hers away and poured the tea.

'There you go.'

'Thanks. Paul—'

'I was ready to go anyway. I left, but I lost my handbag.'

'Jesus!'

'Someone found it, I got it back.'

'Better check the contents,' said Roger. Pauline could see his confidence returning by the second, and realized there was something she had to do before he got it all back and remembered what he'd asked her earlier.

'I'm going to,' she said. 'Hang on a moment.'

She slipped out of the room and went upstairs, carrying her tea and her bag. She went into the bedroom, but thought better of it and went to the bathroom instead, taking her pyjamas and locking the door after her. Then she slipped off her sandals, peeled off the dress and got into the pyjamas. She scrubbed her face, cleaned her teeth and brushed her hair until the transformation was complete. Only then did she sit down on the lavatory seat and drink her tea. Downstairs she could hear the burble of the television. She knew that by doing this – removing the dress, hiding in the bathroom – she was falling well short of her own high standards as a partner, but tonight she simply could not face an aroused and amorous Roger. She hoped that her behaviour would be taken for a small slap on the wrist for the boogieing-in-boxers episode, though truthfully she couldn't have cared less about that. Her hasty departure from the club had had less to do with Roger's behaviour (which she could see had been genuinely forced upon him), than by the disobliging contrast between that and the intense, twilit encounter with Jane Rowe. The contrast had been simply too stark, and she had needed to escape. She only wished – oh, how she wished – that when Jane had met her in the lobby, holding out the lost handbag, she had been able to say something more, something that touched, however inadequately, on her confused and tumultuous feelings. But the door had swung open and Roger and the doorman had been upon her, the wave of her everyday life rolling over them, sweeping them apart, and when she'd next looked, Jane was gone.

Roger watched the late-evening chat show – an actress, a footballer and an author of something the host referred to as 'lad-lit' which Roger suspected was in every sense for the birds – and when Pauline didn't reappear, switched everything off and went upstairs. The lamp on his side of the bed was on and the corner of the duvet flipped back, but Pauline's light was off, and she appeared to be asleep.

Gazing glumly in the bathroom mirror he told himself that he deserved this. There was no excuse for behaving like an idiot in public, especially when he'd come in with the most glamorous woman in the place. The fact that it wasn't like him didn't help either. What had come over him? What had possessed him? Why had he not been man enough to extricate himself? Kelly and her mates had been totally off their faces, how difficult could it have been?

He groaned and rubbed both hands over his face. What a fucking disaster.

Back in the bedroom he slipped into bed as inconspicuously as possible. To his surprise, as he lowered his head gingerly on to the pillow Pauline rolled over and kissed him briefly and bumpily on the cheek, saying sleepily as she did so: 'Night-night.'

His heart leapt, but she was off again, breathing deeply with her back to him, before he had time to respond, let alone capitalize on this concession.

The last thing he registered before turning the light off was the red dress, hanging on the back of the door.

The next morning was Sunday, and they behaved as if everything was back to normal. It was a fine, cold autumn day and Roger got out and cleaned the car thoroughly before getting stuck into some jobs in the garden. The fence needed fresh sealant, and with the sun out, the spare room could wait.

Pauline took her time. After the upheavals of the previous night she needed to catch her breath, get her balance back, restore the status quo. She was change-averse, and didn't care to be shaken or stirred. A calm, sensible, even sort of life was what she preferred, and Roger's bit of party silliness she could have taken in her stride – she had done so, in fact. What she was finding hard to cope with was this sweet sadness, this sense of loss, and longing, that was entirely foreign to her nature.

When she was dressed, in her weekend outfit of brown cords and a pale blue polo-neck, she felt better – more in control. From outside came the small, soothing sounds of Roger, busy making amends. Just for once she herself didn't feel like being busy. There was nothing she wanted to do; she was at once listless, and full of a restless, humming energy. Her evening bag lay on the dressing table where she'd left it last night. She picked it up and sat down on the bed, meaning to restore its contents to her daytime shoulder bag. She noticed that it smelt faintly of the little brown cheroots Jane Rowe had been smoking.

She opened it and shook everything out on to the duvet. Lippie, perfume, eyeliner pencil, tissue, ten-pound note, keys – and what was this? Face down on the broderie anglaise lay a pale grey business card. Pauline picked it up and turned it over. Printed on it in a dashing black copperplate script was the name Jane Rowe, with her address, phone number and email.

The room around Pauline seemed to recede. Her heart pumped wildly, she could feel the blood pulsing and rushing through her veins. But it was with the utmost care and deliberation that she took her wallet from her handbag, and slipped the business card behind her photo of Roger, where it fitted snugly and could not be seen. Then she put the other bits and pieces where they belonged and returned the evening bag to her accessories drawer.

Before leaving the bedroom she put the red dress, on its hanger, in a zip-up, polythene garment cover, and hung it inside the wardrobe behind her winter coat.

When, later on, Roger asked if she fancied a pub lunch, she agreed readily, and they had a really nice time, sitting out in the garden and listening to the jazz band that accompanied the monthly barbecue.

That night Roger – tentatively – made another, more exciting suggestion, and Pauline went along with that, too. Right away he sensed an important but indefinable difference. Pauline was as sweet and accommodating as ever, but seemed curiously absent – distracted, almost, as though her mind were elsewhere. She had never, ever, given Roger cause to be jealous, but this was disconcerting. When it came to the moment, though, she was closer than she'd ever been to letting go, and he went off like a rocket, never better.

When they were lying side by side afterwards, Pauline's head on Roger's shoulder, he said: 'All right, Paul?'

She nodded.

'That was great for me. Fantastic.'

There was no reply, so he added: 'You know how much I love you don't you?'

She didn't answer, but seemed sleepy and peaceful, so he had to assume that she did.

Pauline was there early. Punctuality, it had been drummed into her, in both the professional and private spheres, was the politeness of princes – the very least you could do. But in this instance, being late was simply not an option! She had thought of little else all day, broke the speed limit on the dual carriageway, and flew to the meeting place on winged feet.

Just as well, because the gardens of Glanville House were enormous, and the laurel walk itself about a quarter of a mile from the car park. When – with the aid of the useful free map dispensed by a guide – she arrived, she seemed to be the only person there. On Wednesday evenings the gardens (though not the house) remained open till six, and it was only five fifteen, but there weren't many people around, and

160

most of those were strolling on the terraces or in the rose gardens, enjoying the late afternoon sun. The laurel walk stretched before her, formal and secret between its great square-cut ramparts of dark hedge, the velvet-smooth grass bisected by shadow. There was a hush. She half expected to see a figure in a panniered dress heavy with pearls and a ruff, or another in a cape and feathered hat, sword at his side, cross the path in front of her.

But she was quite alone.

Slowly, now that she was here, she walked down the shallow stone steps and along the path between the high green walls, her footsteps making no sound on the close-cropped grass. At irregular intervals niches had been cut into the hedges and each niche contained its treasure – a sundial, a nymph, a grinning Bacchus, an urn overflowing with trailing flowers. Pauline passed each one by, until she found what she was looking for.

The unicorn stood at right angles to the path, facing outward, one hoof lifted, emerging from the green depths of the hedge as if it had just walked through from the other side. Its neck was proudly arched, and its ears pricked, but the eyes in its beautiful, narrow face, though made of blind white stone, seemed to look directly at Pauline.

This was the sunny side of the path, and she had come straight from work, wearing the prescribed navy suit and white shirt. Now she took off the jacket and dropped it on the ground, rolled up the sleeves of the shirt and slipped off her navy courts.

Then she went over to the unicorn and cautiously, gently, touched its forelock, and the elegantly spiralling horn that grew out of it. She expected the dappled grey and white stone to feel cold, but it didn't: it was warm, and she even laid her forehead against the unicorn's neck for a moment.

'That's better.'

Pauline lifted her head, as Jane Rowe emerged from the shade on the other side of the path – materialized, almost, like the shadow itself made flesh. She wore a sleeveless black dress with a hem that dipped to just above her ankles, and flat black shoes; no jewellery, and no handbag, just a little black leather purse on a cord around her waist. Her arms were pale as a statue's and very lean and shapely.

It was Jane who had spoken, and now she stood a little way off, on the border between light and shade, and said: 'There you are.'

'You were here already,' said Pauline. 'I thought I was early.'

'I was walking around. I like it here.'

'It's lovely.'

Jane came closer, her eyes resting on Pauline.

'You are lovely.'

'Oh, but I'm just ... this is only ... I came from work...'

'Lovely,' repeated Jane. She was now so close that Pauline could smell her thick hair, and see the grain of her unmade-up skin, the hairs that grew vertically at the centre of her black eyebrows, the sea-grey flecks on her irises.

'So are you...' Pauline's voice had sunk to a husky whisper. She scarcely knew herself; she was spellbound.

When Jane touched her it was like flowers blooming inside her, pushing their way to the surface, making her body bud and blossom. Her mouth and Jane's made a single mouth, soft and sweet as ripe peaches.

'What if—?'

'They won't. No one will.'

'Please...'

'Yes.'

'Yes...'

Slowly, the two of them folded and lay down together in the shadow of the unicorn.

When Roger got home to an empty house,

he first checked the diary calendar on the kitchen notice board: nothing there. Maybe – he frowned as he cudgelled his brains – he had forgotten something. It was very unlike Pauline not to say if she was going to be late home. On Tuesday she went swimming, on Thursday she shopped; on Monday it was her Advanced IT lesson, but not until later. She must have been delayed at work – but there was no message on the answering machine or on his mobile voicemail.

It was peculiarly unsettling. They were creatures of habit, he and Pauline, so small inconsistencies and deviations from routine stood out.

Roger poured himself a beer and took it out on to the patio. Almost at once the phone rang and he jumped up – that'd be her.

'Rog?'

His heart gave a slither of disappointment. 'Hi, Kelly.'

'How you doing?'

'Not so bad. Yourself?'

'Better now.'

He laughed grimly. 'A bit rough there for a while, eh?'

'Not many...'

'That's what you get for enjoying your birthday so much.'

'Yeah.' There was a slight pause. 'Rog—'

'What?'

'How's Pauline?'

He found himself glancing around, before saying: 'She's not here at the moment. Not back yet.'

'No, I don't want to speak to her. Just wondered how she was.'

'She's good, thanks.'

'Only she went rushing off, from the party.'

'Yeah, well...' Embarrassed, he rubbed his face and head vigorously with his free hand. 'Never mind.'

'Sorry about all that.'

'That's all right. Only a bit of fun.'

'You didn't do much to stop us.' There was a smile in her voice.

'You're right.'

'Anyway ... As long as Pauline didn't give you a hard time.'

'No, she's cool.' There was another pause and he had already taken the breath that was the preamble to hanging up, when Kelly said: 'She looked amazing.'

'She did, yeah.'

'I mean she always looks smart, Pauline, but I've never seen her go for it like that. You must have been well chuffed.'

'I was. I really was.'

'Okay, Rog.' This time Kelly laughed properly, he didn't know what at. 'I'll let you get on with it. Give my love to Pauline. And thanks for the perfume, it's wicked.'

'No sweat.' It was the first Roger had heard of the perfume. 'And thanks for a great evening.'

She laughed again. 'Don't mention it. Bye.'

'Bye, Kelly.'

Half an hour later he heard Pauline's key in the front door and had to exert a massive effort of willpower not to jump up and rush in and ask her where she'd been. Instead, he called out in a casual voice: 'Hi, Paul!'

'Hi there...! Went for a drink with Trudy, won't be a moment!'

Her footsteps went quickly up the stairs and into the bathroom. The toilet flushed, water ran ... She was quite a while, and then the door clicked and she must have gone into the bedroom, because it was several more minutes before she came down, and she'd changed out of her work clothes into a long cotton skirt and a kaftan-style top.

'Hi...' She kissed him quickly and sat down in the other chair. 'Lovely evening.'

'You look nice,' he said. 'Have I seen that outfit before?'

'I've had them a while.' She looked down

at herself, picking at the fabric as if reminding herself. 'But I've hardly worn them. Not sure they're my style.'

Actually, he knew what she meant. As a rule she looked best in smart, tailored clothes, but this evening the soft, hippyish gear seemed to suit her.

'They are.'

'That's all right then,' said Pauline.

'I haven't done anything about tea, I didn't know where you were.'

'No rush, there's plenty of stuff in the fridge.'

'How was Trudy?'

'Oh, fine...'

'Want a glass of wine?'

'No, thanks.'

Pauline laid her head back and closed her eyes. The evening sun shone on her face. Roger had never known her come in from work and just sit quietly like this, without a care in the world, unconcerned about getting their tea, or about anything, as far as he could see. It was a little unnerving.

'Kelly called,' he said.

'Oh?'

'She sent her love,' he said, which seemed to be the simplest interpretation he could put on the conversation. 'And said thanks for the perfume.'

'Glad she liked it,' said Pauline and then, after quite a long interval asked: 'How was your day?' but so dreamily that he had the impression that it wouldn't much matter how it had been.

'So-so,' he replied, though as a matter of fact it had been quite good. But if he'd been hoping this ambivalent reply might draw her out, he was disappointed.

'Sun's nice,' was all she said.

They sat for a few minutes in silence, enjoying it. Pauline never opened her eyes, and when Roger eventually got up to go and check out the possibilities for supper, he found she was fast asleep.

It was an enchanted sleep, and from that moment on Pauline was living, so she felt, in a dream.

Once or twice a week, as much as she reasonably could without arousing Roger's suspicions, she met Jane. After that first time, beneath the magical protection of the unicorn – for if it wasn't magic, how had they not been discovered? – she went to Jane's cottage, which was in the middle of nowhere, down a long track in the country-side north of town.

'Are you a witch?' she asked, as they lay together one early evening, on the high brass bed in Jane's tiny bedroom. Through the casement window, they had a view of rolling drowsy fields and a line of sentinel trees.

Jane stroked Pauline's hair back from her face and kissed her forehead. 'Not that I know of.'

'You put a spell on me.'

'"I put a spell on you ..."' sang Jane softly, in her deep voice that was uncannily like Nina Simone's original. 'Maybe I did.'

'What am I going to do?' asked Pauline. The question was for herself, really, her tone one not of desperation but of wide-eyed wonderment.

'Why must you do anything? Just be.'

'This can't go on.'

'Why not? Certainly it can. And it probably will. We can't stop it. It would be wicked to stop.'

That one word was like a tiny splinter, pricking Pauline's conscience.

'But perhaps I'm being wicked.'

'Do you think you are?'

'I don't want to hurt Roger.'

'Does he know?'

'No ... No, he's not stupid, he senses something's different, but he doesn't know about us.'

'Then you're not hurting him.'

To think more clearly, Pauline rolled out of Jane's embrace. They lay facing each other, gazing into one another's eyes.

'Be selfish,' said Jane.

'I am being.'

'Who do you want more?'

Pauline noticed that Jane did not say 'love' but 'want'. In answer, she reached out her hand and laid it on Jane's shoulder, and felt, at the same time, Jane's hand on her breast, the thumb grazing her nipple. Her eyes closed.

'And who wants you more?' whispered Jane.

She couldn't reply, because she could not longer reason. The small tangle of conflicting thoughts was drowned out by sensation, and she allowed herself to be drawn into Jane's embrace.

Half an hour later, as she left, Jane said: 'There is something you could do.'

A couple of days later when Roger got home, he thought at first that Pauline wasn't there. This was less rare these days, she'd taken to having a drink with Trudy quite often, and to going to an aromatherapist after work whom she claimed was having a miraculous effect on her stress levels. Roger couldn't argue with that. He'd never known

Pauline so chilled. Odd, then, that this new laid-back Pauline should feel so lost to him. Whatever his private concerns, he'd known where he was with the old one: she was the one he'd taken up with in the first place, and if she was anyone's worst enemy it was her own, not his.

Now there was something going on that he couldn't get a handle on. And whenever he thought he might be about to he shied away and focused on something else. No denying he was in denial. Big-time.

He stood in the narrow hallway, looking and listening. The living room and kitchen doors stood open, and both rooms were pin-neat, untouched, just as they'd left them this morning. Through the kitchen window he could see the tops of the garden chairs leaning, folded, against the sill.

A small sound from above sent him to the foot of the stairs.

'Paul? Paul, that you?'

'Up here...' Her voice sounded distant, as it often did these days, and not only because she was in the bedroom.

Cold and sick, Roger went up the stairs.

The moment, the very second, that he entered the room and she looked up from her packing, he knew. In less than a second he'd taken in her calm face, a silver necklace he hadn't seen before, her eyes which were huge, the pupils dilated like those of a cat in the dark. He was flooded by a long pent-up tidal wave of desolating sadness that was also relief. This was it then.

He began to cry, his shoulders lurching and heaving, tears streaming down his cheeks, his nose running. Pauline opened the second of the small bedside drawers and took out a spotless, ironed handkerchief which she handed to him before quietly returning to her case and zipping the cover. She lifted the case and put it on the ground next to her – it looked light, there wasn't much in there, but Roger took no comfort from that. There was a simple, unadorned finality in Pauline's every movement.

'Roger,' she said. 'I have to go.'

He was still weeping, but he managed to nod, dabbing his eyes and nose with the still-folded handkerchief that smelt of the steam freshener she put in the iron.

'I'm so sorry.'

He raised a helpless hand, both dismissing her apology and fending off her pity.

'You're a wonderful person,' she said. 'I've been so lucky. But there's nothing I can do about this.'

He didn't ask what it was she could do nothing about. He had not the faintest idea, not the tiniest inkling who it might be, and right now he couldn't bear to be told, he was in enough pain as it was.

She picked up the case.

'Don't worry about the car. I'll catch the bus.'

He stared at her. His throat creaked with the strain of holding back sobs.

'I'll be in touch.'

He'd lost the power of movement: instead of stepping aside, he just stood there, shuddering, blocking her way. She had to manoeuvre round him to get out of the small room with her case, and she managed it without so much as touching him. He heard her go down the stairs, take the two steps to the front door, open it ... and close it behind her.

Out in the road, Pauline heard his bellow of agony, and closed her eyes, for only a moment, as she walked away.

The bus route went past Planet Shopping. She thought she could see herself, neat and businesslike, bag over her shoulder marching briskly across the car park to do her weekly shop: an alien.

An hour later, as she walked up the unmade

road, she rounded a bend and saw the cottage in the distance. She had not told Jane of her intentions, she did not even know if she'd be welcome. This was something she had never done before, nor thought herself capable of doing: a leap into the unknown. In spite of her sore feet she felt light as a feather, buoyant and empty as a balloon. Free as air.

Almost there now. And as she approached, the door opened.

'I say, Joan, have you seen this?' Pat asked her fellow Tuesday-lady in the charity shop.

'Good heavens!' Maureen started in mock-astonishment, and then fingered the dress. 'It's rather fab, though ... Who brought that in?'

'That young bloke, the cute one, you commented...'

'Oh, yes, what a doll!'

'This was right at the bottom of his bag of stuff.' Pat hung the dress on the hook behind the counter and the two women stood gazing at it admiringly.

'I'd buy it myself,' said Maureen, 'only I'd need to be on Atkins for a year.'

'I think the window, don't you? Make a bit of a splash?'

'Definitely.'

'Price?' asked Pat. 'What do you reckon?'
'That sort of glamour?' remarked Maureen. 'Priceless!'

Jasper

Yesss! Result! They'd stuffed them! Cream-
ed them! Whupped their poxy posh arses,
wiped them off the park!

The whole fucking coach was going crazy,
even Mr Mather was looking a bit pleased
and pretending not to notice stuff. The lads
swiped portholes in the steamed-up win-
dows just so they could see the expressions
on the other motorists' faces as the conquer-
ing heroes of Clayborne College cruised
victoriously down the motorway.

Dobbo, Micky and Jasper were sat at the
back, playing it cool as befitted the archi-
tects of a famous victory. Dobbo had been
rock-solid in goal during an edgy first-half,
Mickey had played a Rooney-esque blinder
in mid-field and Jasper had set up one goal
and scored another two – one of them the
penalty of the century, worthy of Beckham
at his banana-ing best.

'So where we going tonight then?' asked
Dobbo.

'George?' suggested Micky, a reference to the area's most youth-friendly pub.

Dobbo checked with Jasper. 'George all right?'

'Dunno,' said Jasper. 'Let me know where you are and I'll turn up if I can.'

Mickey peered round at Jasper with a lascivious smirk. 'Got better things to do, then?'

'No!' said Jasper with a testy, upward inflection. 'No!'

Dobbo joined in with the smirking. 'How is Rachel Worboys these days?'

'Fuck off.'

'Ooo-ooh!' chorused the other two.

In the college car park the parents' cars were lined up on the far side and a group of parents were standing together, chatting. They all looked round and stared expectantly at the coach as it rolled in, but by common consent none of the lads gave the game away; they all sat slumped in their seats, nonchalant and blank-faced.

Mr Mather got off first, and must have given the waiting parents the thumbs-up, because they all whooped and jumped up and down and one or two of them hugged one another – Jasper noticed Dobbo's old man getting a cheap feel of Clive Pack's

177

Mum. Couldn't blame him, she was pretty fit, though Jasper knew (it was the cross he had to bear) that his own mother headed the league table of MILTF.

They trooped off, thanking the driver who was the usual grumpy sod, completely impervious to the privilege and honour that was his. Coach drivers and caretakers, thought Jasper, there was a farm somewhere that turned them out – the hairstyles, the clothes, the attitude problem, the BO...

As he got to the bottom of the steps Mr Mather slapped him on the shoulder.

'Good stuff, Jasper.'

This was high praise, and however much they all moaned, they rated Mather. As teachers went, he was pretty cool. Jasper scowled.

'Thanks sir.'

Jasper was getting a lift home with Dobbo. His dad was classic.

'Fantastic lads! Magic! Want to stop at the shop?'

'Yeah...' They nodded.

Mr Dobbin passed a fiver over his shoulder between his index and middle fingers, like a cigarette.

'Anything you want! That's legal and decent!' He chuckled matily. Dobbo and

Jasper avoided each other's eyes. Mr Dobbin was okay but majorly embarrassing.

After they'd been in the shop and were heading homeward with their spoils – a haul of sweets, cans of Dr Pepper and two computer mags, one with a free demo disc – Mr Dobbin adopted a more serious, man-to-man tone.

'Wish I'd been there. Who scored the goals?'

'He did,' said Dobbo.

'Jasper?' Mr Dobbin craned to look in the mirror. 'You did?'

'Two of them.'

'And he set up the third.'

'Top man! What about the opposition, good as you expected?'

'Not bad,' conceded Jasper. 'Tested us a bit in the first half hour, but second half we were all over them.'

'Competitive?'

'Animals,' said Dobbo. 'I got a right clattering from the gorilla on the wing.'

'There's always one, son,' agreed Mr Dobbin, more in sorrow than in anger. 'There's always one...'

But Jasper knew how to push all Mr Dobbin's buttons.

'Never mind, eh,' he said. 'You should have seen the other guy.'

179

'Right!' Mr Dobbin guffawed and slapped his hand on the wheel. 'Right you are!'

Jasper let himself in at the front door and dropped his kit bag in the hall. At once, his mother appeared at the top of the stairs, barefoot in her joggers and a towelling hoodie.

'Hi! How did you get on?'

'Thrashed them.'

'Brilliant.' She pattered down the stairs and gave him a kiss. 'What's all this?'

'Dobbo's dad gave us a fiver.'

'I see you spent it wisely...' She gave him a playful slap on the arm to show she didn't mind this time. 'Look, sorry Jass, but your father and I are going to that business thing tonight. He's running a bit late so I'm meeting him there. There's a pasta bake on the side, just give it a couple of minutes in the microwave.'

'Cheers. What flavour?'

'Creamy basil and tomato with extra cheese. Made with my own fair hand.'

'Wicked.'

'Sorry,' she said again, and then pulled an apologetic grimace and hugged him. 'Ooh ... Jass ... What a shame. You have a great win and we're not here to celebrate.'

'I don't mind,' he said truthfully. He liked

having the place to himself, and his mother's slight guilt meant she was being extra nice to him and would probably go on being tomorrow for a while till the effect wore off. Not that she was a heavy parent, but it was always nice to have the sympathy vote.

'Now look,' she said, 'I've got to dash. Put that lot in the machine and leave the boots in the utility room, okay?'

'Okay.'

'Are you going out later?'

'Don't know, I might.'

'If you do,' she said, 'remember we'll have had a drink so you'll have to get yourself back.'

'Sure.'

'And in by twelve, yes?'

'Yes, yes...' He pretended to be grumpy, but she knew he wasn't really, and ruffled his head before pattering away up the stairs ruffling her wet hair with her hands.

Not long after Jasper's mother had left, when he was stuffing his football kit into the machine, Dobbo called.

'You coming out?'

'No.'

'Why not? Go on, it's Saturday.'

'I'm knackered.'

'So? We can get some dope from Biggsy, chill out.'

'No Dobbs, I told you, I don't feel like it.'

'You all right?' Dobbo sounded suspicious.

'Of course I'm all right.'

'So—'

'I can't be arsed, okay?' said Jasper, firmly but without rancour.

This answer seemed to satisfy Dobbo, who let the subject of this evening go. 'Kick around tomorrow morning?'

'Might do.'

'Seeya.'

'Cheers Dobbo.'

When he'd finished speaking to Dobbo, Jasper put his muddy boots in the utility room, drew the curtains front and back and checked the latches were up on both doors. Then he laid the table. He put out a table mat, a white linen serviette, and the two spiral glass candlesticks off the side, the ones his mother used when she gave a dinner party. There were candles already in them, the ivory non-drip ones, part used, no one was going to notice another half-hour's wear. He laid a knife and fork, and added a pudding spoon and a side plate just because they looked nice, and one of the long-stemmed wine goblets to complete the picture.

Then he went upstairs and began running a bath with a generous dash of Culpeper's bath oil. His mother kept some scented tea-lights for when she wanted to have a real wallow, and he lit a couple of those and placed them at either end. His father's swanky black rubber shower radio was on the Norwegian slate shelf next to the freestanding glass basin (he'd seen the shiny catalogues), his hand hovered over the radio for a moment but he didn't switch it on.

In the bedroom he stripped off quickly, threw his shirt, socks and boxers into the corner and draped his school uniform over the chair, with the tie still knotted, ready for Monday. There was a mirror on the landing and he tried not to look at his skinny, white, mud-stained self as he scampered across, pausing only to grab a clean towel out of the airing cupboard.

In the bathroom he locked the door, and turned off the taps. Then he stepped in, slowly lowering each foot, then his backside, through the fragrant, steaming foam into the exquisitely hot water. Just as slowly, savouring every scalding, scented inch, he lay back, and let out a long sigh of pleasure and relief.

Now, at last, he could relax. No music, he revelled in the sequestered quiet, broken only by the occasional gentle gloop and splash as he sponged his arms and legs, and the distant sounds from outside of less fortunate, busy people, doing stuff.

He stayed in the bath for over half an hour, occasionally topping up the heat, until it was too full to add any more. Then he washed all over, including his hair, climbed out and dried himself thoroughly with the soft, clean towel, dropping it in the laundry basket when he'd finished. In the corner of the bathroom was a whicker shelf unit loaded with nice, expensive toiletries: his mother liked a choice. He selected a lily of the valley body lotion, and rubbed it on all over. Afterwards, his skin felt smooth as silk, and smelt wonderful. Finally, he cleaned his teeth. Before leaving the bathroom he rinsed out the bath and basin fastidiously, and hung the bathmat over the heated rail.

Then, naked and reborn, Jasper walked into his parents' bedroom.

He loved it in here: the luxurious thick carpet, the stylishly swagged, asymmetric curtains, so luxurious that they puddled on the floor, the oriental cushions scattered at the head of the bed – the bold, unashamed sensuality of it all. His parents were still hot for each other, a fact which Jasper found encouraging as well as deeply embarrassing.

He sensed that this was why his mother could respond playfully and flirtatiously to all the other men – his friends' fathers among them – who came on to her. She was confident. She didn't need anyone else.

Jasper gave himself a moment to enjoy the room. Although the window overlooked the garden, he drew the curtains just to feel the heavy swish and pull of the textured fabric, and turned on a couple of the uplighters so that a soft, pink glow fanned out over the walls. Then he lay down on the bed. The bedspread was embroidered silk, cool and smooth under his bare skin. Speculatively, he touched himself. Already he was beginning to harden in anticipation.

After a couple of minutes he got off the bed. All his movements were slow, he liked to take these moments at a ritualistic pace. One by one he opened the drawers in his mother's chest of drawers, each a little further than the last so that he could see what was there; they slid out smooth as silk on their runners, revealing their gorgeous bounty, the colour of sugared almonds, roses, butterfly wings ... Jasper gasped – every time, every fucking time it was so amazing he could hardly breathe...

Heart pounding, he pushed his hand into the top drawer, among the petals of silk, the feathers of lace, the trickle of ribbons and the rich, creamy slither of satin, and drew out slippery, flared French knickers in apricot, trimmed with tiny pearl and apricot rosebuds.

Slowly, shivering with pleasure, Jasper drew them on. And reached once more into the drawer.

After the kick-around next morning the three of them went to the George.

'You lazy bastard,' said Dobbo. 'You missed a good night.'

'Large one, was it?'

'Yeah.' Dobbo glanced meaningfully at Micky. 'You could say that.'

Micky grimaced. 'What are you looking at?'

'He was trolleyed,' said Dobbo.

'What, and you weren't, is that it?'

Dobbo gave a nonchalant one-shouldered shrug. 'Some of us can hold our drink, some of us can't.'

'Sorry I missed it,' said Jasper.

'So what did you get up to? Adult Friend Finder and a box of tissues?'

'Fuck off.'

'Hold up,' said Micky, rolling his eyes. 'Rachel's in.'

Dobbo slid his eyes in the same direction.

186

'Very nice. Don't fancy yours though.'

'Every bird's best accessory,' said Micky. 'A plug-ugly friend.'

They were being unfair. Jasper didn't think the friend was plug-ugly, it was just that not many of the girls around here looked as good as Rachel, who was a five-star, card-carrying, ocean-going babe. This morning she was busy seeing off the competition in a plain black singlet, faded jeans and Nikes.

'Don't let us stop you,' said Dobbo.

'Won't be a minute.'

'And the rest...'

The thing about Rachel was, she wasn't just hot, she was really really nice. She didn't play games. In fact (this was something Jasper kept strictly to himself and hoped would never be discovered) she reminded him a bit of his mother. She was a looker and she had the same cheerful, charming confidence. She'd never knowingly hurt anyone so no one was likely to hurt her. For some unfathomable reason she did seem to have a soft spot for him, and he had a distinctly hard spot for her.

'Hi, Jass!' She put one arm round his neck and kissed him. 'Congratulations!'

'Thanks.'

'This is Marie.'

'Hi.'

'Hi,' said Marie. 'I'm going to talk to Lisa.'

'Catch you later,' said Rachel, and then turned back to Jasper. 'You scored the goals, right?'

'Couple of them.'

'Brilliant. Wish we'd been allowed to come.'

'Yeah, we could have done with some cheerleaders.'

'I'm going to suggest it to Mather for next season!' she declared, and then frowned with disappointment. 'Only there won't be a next season, will there?'

'Fair point.'

They fell silent for a moment. Beyond the great rampart of this summer's GCSEs stretched the unknown terrain of sixth-form college, work, training, whatever they went for or could get into. Rachel knew what she was going to do, the one-year diploma in Health and Beauty at the CFE. She'd already done work experience in a top salon, and needed hardly any GCSEs to get on to the course. She had a life plan – her own business in three years. She seemed to combine, in one gorgeous package, all the best things about being both a teenager and an adult. Jasper envied her certainty. Beyond struggling through the exams he had no idea what he wanted. If he got the grades, he might take a couple of A-levels just to buy himself a bit more time, but that was by no means guaranteed. He was full of a huge, vague, unfocused yearning but couldn't have said what for.

'So,' said Rachel, tucking a silken swathe of brown hair behind one ear, 'were you celebrating last night?'

He thought about this, but only for a moment. 'Yes.'

She leaned forward confidentially, cutting her eyes at Dobbo and Micky. 'You look better than those two.'

'Oh well,' he said, 'some of us can hold our drink and some of us can't.'

Rachel laughed. 'Fancy sitting outside?'

As they went out, he caught a faint ribald cheer from the corner of the bar, and took no notice.

It was fresh in spite of the sun, but Jasper was warmed by the simple fact of being out here, the bloke Rachel wanted to be sitting outside with. When she leaned forward to tweak something off her shoe he caught a glimpse of her bra, black with a broderie anglaise trim.

A propos of nothing at all, she said, 'Marie's okay, actually.'

'Yeah, she seemed – okay.'

'She's working on losing the weight. She's started coming to Jazzercise, I'm so proud of her.'

'Right.' There were some girlie expressions Jasper had never been able to get a handle on, and this was one of them. Why would Rachel be 'so proud' of her fat, plain friend? It wasn't as if she had any responsibility for her, she wasn't her mother, or her teacher. He didn't get it.

'What's jazzercise?'

'Jazz dance. Exercise. Jazzercise.'

'Oh, yeah – right.'

Come on Jasper, he thought despairingly, get your arse in gear. You're sat outside with the officially most-fancied girl in the area, at her invitation, and you're not exactly showing her a good time.

'You look great,' he said.

'Do I?' She looked down at herself and laughed. 'Thanks! I haven't made what you'd call a humungous effort.'

'You don't need to.'

'Oh Jass...' She pulled a face that expressed, charmingly, a kind of agonized, humorous appreciation. 'You're so sweet.'

'No,' he said, warming to this theme, 'it's true. You do look better than anyone else. The belt's fab.'

'I love it to bits. I got it in Topshop...' She

ran her fingers along the belt and then looked up at him shyly. 'I can't believe you talk about clothes like that.'

'Like what?'

'Well – talk about them at all, really. Most boys don't.'

'Don't they?' He felt suddenly nervous, as if he were about to give himself away, his secret let out.

'No! They don't care, they just know what they like.'

'Me too.'

She shook her head. 'It's not the same. You really notice.'

'I notice you,' said Jasper, desperate to make this about her rather than his own personal quirks.

Such was his discomfort with the subject that he was actually pleased when Rachel glanced past his shoulder and said: 'Here's Marie.'

When Jasper got back from the George at half past three, it was to find his father mowing the grass – sure sign the football season was ending – and his mother in the kitchen, caught in a kind of freeze frame with her naked-woman apron (a present from him) looped round her neck, but not tied at the back, a kitchen knife in her hand,

and the telephone handset held to her ear with the other. She waggled the knife at him in greeting, but continued talking as he opened the fridge and took out a J_20.

'...rather play a singles than mess about with only three people, do you think we're up for that?' She laughed loudly at the answer. 'Let's do it then, you're booked for a thrashing, Tuesday at seven ... Yes! ... You bet ... Bye.'

'Sheila...' She put the handset down on the windowsill and sent him a wry smile as if he'd been in on both sides of the conversation. 'We're going to play a singles, I must be mad, I'm so not in her league.'

'You'll sort her out, no worries,' said Jasper. So intense was his relief that he had successfully covered his tracks that he considered going over and kissing her except that might have aroused her suspicions.

'Ah, bless you...' She tied the apron and turned her attention to new potatoes on the chopping board. 'Been at the George?'

'Yes.'

'How's Rachel?' She didn't turn round and her tone was super-casual, but Jasper still felt the prickle of maternal curiosity.

'She wasn't there.'

He wandered to the window and stood next to her, looking out at his father.

'We'll eat around five,' she said.

'Fine. What are we having?'

'Lamb?'

'Not twiggy—'

'No rosemary, no, I remembered.'

'Cheers, Mum.'

'And just in case you're wondering— ' she nudged him affectionately with her elbow – 'these aren't the only potatoes.'

'Roasties?'

'In there as we speak.'

'Wicked.'

'Go out and say hallo to Dad, he hasn't seen you since the match, and he could do with an excuse to stop.'

'Okay.'

Jasper went out of the side door. Their house was a big, sixties-built place with a chalet roof, and his parents had extended it some years ago. In the angle of the kitchen and the utility room was a square of basic patio (as opposed to the expensive and attractive granite crazy paving by the lounge), where the circular dryer stood. This afternoon its arms were hung about with Jasper's soccer kit, his school stuff, and the fluffy primrose-yellow towel he'd used last night. Fortunately, his mother was used to his profligacy with towels so it hadn't provoked any unwelcome comment.

He wandered to the edge of the lawn and stood there a little self-consciously until his father spotted him and closed down the engine.

'Morning!'

'Hi, Dad.'

Jasper's father came over, raising an arm to wipe his brow on the shoulder of his T-shirt. 'What's all this I hear about trouncing Longfield three–nil?'

'We did, yeah.'

Jasper had heard his father described – by one of his mother's friends – as 'an alpha male'. It was a good description. His father was big, fit, handsome, a bit overpowering, really. Until ten years ago he'd been a useful rugby player, and Jasper couldn't help sensing a trace of disapproval towards the sissier, yobbier, overpaid game at which his son excelled.

'Well done.' He put his arm round Jasper's shoulders and gave him a manly squeeze that nearly cracked several ribs. 'And you were the goal scorer?'

'Yes – well, one of them.'

'What a hero! We were really sorry not to be around last night. I hope you managed to celebrate without us.'

'Yes.' Jasper made an 'and how!' face and his father chuckled.

'I could use a beer, how about you?'

'No thanks.' Jasper raised his J$_2$O. 'I'm all right.'

'Back in a tick – take a pew, I want to hear all about it.'

Jasper sat down on one of the wicker chairs with the fat, pink and white cushions. Drink was one of several areas where his father – well, both his parents, but especially his father – seemed to be ambivalent, or at least to have entered into some kind of un-acknowledged collusion with each other and with him. In a rural area like this there wasn't a lot for the young to do, and certain publicans were known to be youth-friendly but sensible. It was as though his parents had agreed between themselves to turn a blind eye to the underage drinking, the sex (not yet an issue in Jasper's case) and even possibly the dope (they couldn't, surely, not know about the dope), in order to keep their powder dry for when they might really need it. Indeed Jasper recognized that his father regarded a spot of drinking and womaniz-ing, especially when associated with sport-ing triumphs, to be if not obligatory then entirely in order. It was a pity, in a way, about the lack of sex. He didn't think he was the only one, though. Micky was crafty and secretive, he had probably done it, but

195

Dobbo was a fully paid-up bullshitter and almost certainly a virgin.

Still, all that was by the by. The one thing Jasper's father could never, ever have guessed at – and it was Jasper's unceasing fervent prayer that he never would – was what made Jasper truly, ecstatically, happy.

Now he came back, carrying an old-fashioned glass tankard with a handle, foaming to the brim, and sat down on the other chair.

'So,' he said. 'Give me the whole story. Spare no detail, relive the whole thing.'

Later that evening, Jasper went upstairs to his room and logged on. While the machine booted up he put the usual safeguards in place: his GCSE Maths revision book, notebook and biro on the desk next to the mouse pad. He typed in the special website, something he wouldn't usually have done when they were in, and awake, but right now they were subject to the voluntary pin-down which was the Sunday night natural history programme, so he considered himself pretty safe for at least three quarters of an hour.

Up it came. And suddenly Jasper was in another world, a more real world, where there were no fears and tensions, where everyone was like him, and eager to be his friend. There were the familiar web-names – Gloria, Sylvie, Louette – and in no time at all he was picking up tips and messages and posting his own back.

Great slingbacks, big sizes, at Shoe Warehouse, Withershaw Retail Park off A14...
Have you tried the Diva catalogue for pretty tops and easy skirts?
Ball gowns with balls...
Peta and Robyn do beautiful, feminine hair...

Last night's had been a lonely ecstasy, and one that was tinged, as always, with the sickening fear of discovery. Now, the bright screen was like a sunlit window on to a world where hundreds – thousands – of happy, friendly, well-adjusted people greeted him and others, confided in one another, chatted and joked. A world where he belonged and was at home. A place of safety, where he could stroll, and be acknowledged and accepted.

He cruised around the website for about ten minutes just revelling in the normality of it all. The best thing about it was that many – most, probably – of these blokes, would be big, sporty, successful, heterosexual middle-aged men like his father, or Dobbo's dad (well, maybe not). Alpha males. Not gay (though there was nothing wrong with that, of course), not effeminate, or kinky; just men who liked to wear beautiful things. He allowed himself to do something he'd not done before, which was to think about Rachel as he cruised, and try to imagine what her reaction would be if he were to tell her. She was so gorgeous, and so mature ... who knows? Jasper pictured a scene where they were on their own, in this house, and he left her alone for a moment and then came down the stairs in all his finery, and she said, 'Oh, Jass...! You never said! You look fabulous – I've got some lovely sparkly earrings that would go with that.' After this romantic moment they'd sit down together on the sofa and talk girl-stuff, and it would bring them closer together, and one thing would lead to another...

Jasper sighed, shuddered, and closed his eyes.

When he opened them again it was to the endlessly spiralling heavenly bodies on his screen-saver. He clicked, and there it was: the invitation. It must have arrived while he was daydreaming and now it sat there, framed, in the middle of the screen as if addressed to him and him alone.

Spring into Summer at Oldthorpe Manor
14–15th May

A weekend of fashion and fun among friends, in the country club described by *The Sunday Times* as 'a dream of English hospitality'.

Shop in relaxed and luxurious surroundings – swim in the heated pool – let yourself be pampered by experts in the unrivalled spa – get advice from the professionals on everything from skincare to accessories – Gary Southern, one of the UK's top motivational speakers on Style, Soul and Self-Esteem.

Two days of pure pleasure for only £200 or either Saturday or Sunday (non-residential) for only £75. Don't miss out! Places are limited, so book now.

There followed all the usual contact details. Jasper read and re-read the invitation (he couldn't help seeing it like that although he knew it was nothing but an advert, really). Two hundred pounds was out of the question, but seventy-five, that was do-able, even allowing for the train fare:

he'd got twice that saved from trolley-wallying at the superstore. He clicked on the hotel's website. Oldthorpe Manor was in Suffolk, and 'within easy reach' of Bury St Edmunds. Plus, there was a 'courtesy bus' to and from the mainline station morning and evening both days. He supposed that meant it was free. Jasper's brain raced: he could do that in a day, no sweat. From here to Bury on the train was only an hour, with one change, if he left at around half past eight and walked to the station ... Yes. And he could be back some time in the evening. The only problem would be thinking up a credible alibi.

'Jasper!'

At the sound of his mother's voice he broke out in a sweat and banged the exit button. She was already coming up the stairs! He opened the Maths revision-aid and grabbed the notebook and biro. The fucking screen finally cleared as she knocked on the door.

'Yeah?'

'Jass?'

'It's open.'

She came in.

'How's it going?'

'Not so bad.'

'You missed a treat, actually, he was talking about marine mammals – amazing film of blue whales...'

She came over and looked over his shoulder, touching his head gently as she did so. She was wearing her Kenzo perfume, the one out of the slender curved bottle that looked like a flower-stem.

'The awful truth is I can't understand a word of that.'

'Just as well you don't have to, then.'

'Good point.' She laughed. 'Are you going to take a break? It's that cop thing you like.'

'I'll give it a miss, thanks. Probably turn in soon.'

'That's not a bad idea. School tomorrow.' She gave his head a little pat and moved away. 'Anything I can get you?'

'No thanks.'

'Night-night then.'

'Night, Mum.'

She closed the door quietly after her. Jasper experienced a small, sharp pang – a mixture of remorse, and guilt, and straightforward love for his mother. He knew how lucky he was. His parents were cool. They didn't nag, they trusted him, they treated him pretty much like an adult. If there was any way he could have not had a secret from them, he'd have taken it like a shot. Maybe one day ... but that day was so far off, and so unimaginable, that he couldn't get his head round it.

Once he'd heard her go all the way back downstairs, he went through the motions of going to bed – used the bathroom, opened and closed doors, played a bit of music so they could hear it. Then he turned the music off and went back on the computer.

The Spring into Summer booking form was pretty prescriptive. You had to be over eighteen for a start, but that wasn't too much of a problem – most of the activities that he and his mates engaged in involved passing themselves off as two or three years older than they were, and he'd never been rumbled yet. Another problem was the deposit. He had no card or cheque book. Then it came to him – if ever there was a situation where the truth – if not the whole truth – would do, this was it. He'd quite simply download the form and send it registered post, with the cash, and a note saying he was sure they'd understand that he wanted his booking to be non-traceable and private.

Pleased to have solved that one, he logged off and got into bed. He didn't read, or even listen to his iPod, but turned out the light and lay with his hands behind his head, gazing at the ceiling and buzzing with excitement. He was still wide awake an hour later when his parents came upstairs, talking quietly. On the landing outside his room they dropped their voices out of respect for his post-revision exhaustion. A few minutes later the chink of light under the door was doused, and everything was quiet. No creak of bedsprings on a Sunday night.

Just as he was about to fall asleep he thought of one drawback – by the time he'd paid for the day and the travel, there'd be very little cash left for shopping.

The moment he'd sent off the form another petrifying possibility occurred to him: he'd put his home address, and the post usually arrived after he'd left for school and before his mother left for her job at the Hospice office. He hoped to God they'd send the confirmation of his booking discreetly, without stuff emblazoned all over the envelope, or there were bound to be questions. He rehearsed what he might say:

'Bloody junk mail!' like his father and sling it in the bin. But then he'd have to catch the first opportunity to fish it out again before it was consigned to the bigger bin outside and got completely saturated with cold tea, gravy, and virgin olive oil.

In the end he struck lucky. Four days after

he'd despatched the form, as he walked to the bus stop, he actually saw the post van parked up the road.

'Anything for Number Three, The Chase?' he asked.

'Let's have a look ... There we go.' The postman handed him three envelopes. 'Expecting something?'

'Yeah.'

'Don't lose them, will you?'

'I'll put them inside now.'

As he went back he had a quick shufti, found the one he wanted and slipped it in his blazer pocket. The other two he was about to push through the letter box when his mother opened the door.

'Whoa – Jass! You gave me a fright, did you forget something?'

'No ... Postman saw me and gave me these.'

'Bills, bills...' She glanced at the envelopes, then used them to shoo him away. 'Quick then, or you'll miss the bus.'

It was a long day for Jasper. But at least the announcement of the league champion-ship in assembly meant that everyone, staff and pupils, was in a good mood. Especially Mr Mather, who was quite choked up, saying how proud everyone should be of the team, and referring to them as 'heroes', who showed 'real character'.

Rachel and her two friends Claire and Shereen sought out Jasper, Dobbo and Micky at lunchtime and demanded that they sit down and watch the cheerleader routine they'd worked out. They rolled the tops of their skirts over till they were barely decent and really went for it, kicking, twirling and chanting, attracting quite a crowd and getting a huge cheer at the end.

'What do you reckon?' asked Rachel. 'Worth a go?'

This got another cheer, but in the middle of it Mr Mather appeared and said with a benign smile that he was sorry to break up the party but this was neither the time nor the place.

'Seriously, sir,' said Rachel, adjusting her skirt. 'You should think about it for next year.'

'We'll see. Now inside the lot of you.'

'I tell you what,' said Dobbo as they shuffled into Citizenship, 'with that much pussy on the touchline who's going to be able to run?'

'Wanker!' said Micky.

'You took the word right out of my mouth.'

But Jasper liked the idea of the cheerleaders. It was a pity they'd all have left, because he could see Rachel already, in a blue and yellow leotard (the college colours), with ra-ra frills, short white socks and pom-poms on her wrists and ankles, her hair in one of those high pony tails, decorated with another pom-pom...

'Jasper,' said Mrs Mumford in her tired voice, 'when you're ready.'

Today was one of the two days a week when he got home before his mother. He made himself a cheese and marmite sandwich and a brew and took them upstairs to his room, turning on his music so that when she did get in she'd know he was there, and not come bursting in looking for washing or old cereal bowls.

He put his RE revision books on the desk, and took the envelope out of his blazer pocket. To be fair it was perfectly discreet, with nothing more than the Oldthorpe Manor logo on the back, but if anything that would have made it more suspicious, and much harder to dismiss as junk mail. He was more than ever grateful that he'd managed to waylay the postman.

He ate one half of his sandwich and drank some of his tea, and then opened the envelope. It was all so wonderfully simple he could have wept with relief and gratitude: an elegant white card, this time produced to look exactly like a personal invitation, with his name handwritten at the top, and then all the information in beautiful curly printed script. At the bottom was written: 'Admission is by invitation only – please bring yours with you.'

Would he ever!

He put the card in the one place he knew no one would come across it – in the inside, zip-up pocket of his school bag – and opened the RE reviser. But some time later when his mother arrived home he was still gazing, unseeing, at the same page.

Later on, at supper, she slid him a teasing glance and said: 'You look happy.'

'Do I?' He at once struggled for an air of sardonic cool.

'That's more like it,' said his father. 'Back to normal.'

'How was school?' asked his mother.

'Not bad.'

'I hope you got three rousing cheers for that result on Saturday,' said his father.

'Yeah – yeah, we did.' This reminded him of something he knew would amuse them. 'Some of the girls did a cheerleader routine.'

'What?' His mother laughed delightedly. 'In assembly?'

'No, in break.'

'Which girls? Rachel?'

'Her and some of her mates.'

'I bet that livened things up,' said his father, who liked Rachel.

'It did.'

'British soccer could do with a bit more of that – glamour, fun, music, pretty girls on the touchline. Too much money and no sense of humour never helped anyone.'

'Anyway,' said Jasper, 'we'll none of us be there next season, so someone else'll have to do it.'

'Sad in a way,' said his mother in a wistful voice. 'Your little gang all going off in different directions.'

'That's life,' said his father, in full philosophical mode. 'Nothing stands still, especially when you're young.' He gave Jasper a rueful, man to man smile. 'It's your world, so make the most of it.'

Jasper realized that in order for his alibi to have authenticity, he should sow the seeds in good time. Not overdo it – that would arouse suspicion – but simply mention it, or the possibility of it, in passing.

A week later, over a takeaway curry with his father (his mother was at a tennis club committee meeting), he said casually: 'Do you remember Danny?'

'Danny who?'

'He used to be at school, that very tall kid with the Irish accent.' The fictional Danny was fleshing out nicely. Jasper's father furrowed his brow.

'No ... Should I?'

'He moved. He says the new place sucks.'

'What, the school?'

'The whole thing, he can't stand it.'

'Poor old Danny...' Jasper's father slapped his midriff. 'That rogan josh has got your name on it.'

'Cheers.'

Jasper left it at that for the time being. Over the next three weeks he found, interestingly, that excitement and anticipation didn't upset his concentration as much as he feared. In fact it was as if having this fabulous adventure to look forward to actually helped. It gave him something to work towards. His first exam, Art, was only two days after the Spring into Summer weekend, but that required no revision, he'd done well in the course work and was reasonably confident.

One thing did concern him, though: what to wear. By the time he'd paid the balance of the entry fee, and his travel, there'd be nothing left for the much vaunted 'carefree shopping'. At the same time, the whole point of the weekend was to be oneself, to make a statement. And Jasper owned precisely nothing. All the clothes he'd enjoyed wearing were his mother's, and she would certainly notice if half a dozen of her nicest things went missing.

This, he realized, was the main problem that he and thousands of others faced. His skin shrank at the prospect of going into a women's clothes shop and attempting to buy something for himself. The sheer cringe-making embarrassment didn't bear thinking of. And then, more materially, there was the expense. He couldn't afford to buy new things. His mother was a size ten and he could wear her stuff, but here at home he could try things on in front of the long mirror, twirl, tweak and walk back and forth to see whether they suited him or looked totally stupid and ridiculous.

Ironically it was his mother who gave him the idea. The next day he was late, and she offered to run him in. There was a full binbag in the footwell of the car on the passenger side, and she said: 'Oh, chuck that in the back, I've been having a clear-out.'

He chucked, and would have thought no more of it had she not added, looking over her shoulder as she backed out of the drive: 'I'm taking it to the Hospice warehouse.

Some of it's as good as new, and at least I know the people there will sort through and make sure the best things are separated out, it's all in a good cause after all...'

Her vague, inconsequential tone implied that she was more or less talking to herself, and that it was of no possible interest to Jasper. But the following Saturday he took the bus into town and went to the charity shop.

Not the Hospice one, though he was sorely tempted. His mother's clothes were perfect, but he couldn't risk bringing any of them back into the house after she'd thrown them out. Instead he went to the slightly smaller mental health outlet further up the road. The beady eyes of the middle-aged woman behind the till followed him as he assiduously studied the books and DVDs, you could tell she thought everyone under twenty had criminal tendencies and needed watching. But then a couple of other people came in and one of them wanted to try things on, so her attention was diverted.

He flicked idly through the rails, but found it dispiriting. The clothes were clean and pressed, and arranged in order of size and style – trousers, tops and so on – but there was no getting away from their essential dullness and limpness. There was a strong air of the things being just out of date, which was altogether different from the wit and glamour of vintage stuff, even from the seventies. Last year's New Look was old, and M&S was so not his ... He sighed.

'Can I help at all?' asked the woman.

This, then, was the moment – but he'd been thinking about it.

'Looking for something for my girlfriend.'

The woman's expression softened. 'Ah, well ... don't you think she's going to want something new? Have you tried Accessorise?'

He shook his head. 'She likes to be different.'

'I see...' The woman smiled indulgently. 'And you're broke?'

'Pretty much.'

She was on his side now, which was okay in one way, but crap in another because she shadowed him, making helpful suggestions (not!) so he couldn't think. Also, he was absolutely bricking himself in case one of his friends should be walking down the street and spot him pottering about with this over-solicitous granny-figure.

In the end he blurted out: 'Thanks – I've got to go.' And fled.

'Hope you find what you want...!' she

called after him.

And then of course, when he was outside on the pavement, he did! Earlier, he'd been in such a hurry to get inside without being seen, scurrying along with his head down, he'd never noticed what was right in front of him, hanging against a screen in the window. A dress of such jaw-dropping, drop-dead, fuck-off gorgeousness that he could almost feel the slither of the satin on his skin, its smooth embrace around his torso and thighs. And the colour! It seemed to give off a vibration, a hum, a siren song intended for him and him alone. His face burned as he stood there gazing at it, his mouth actually watered. He was transported.

'Back again?' said the woman. 'Seen something you like?'

'The dress in the window—'

'The slinky red number? You think she'll like that?'

'I'll take it.' He was itching now to have the dress, bagged up, in his hand, and be out of here. 'How much?'

'Ten pounds.' The woman made an apologetic face. 'You've got good taste, it's the most expensive item here.'

'Okay.'

'Hand-made,' she added, as though he

gave a stuff.

'Ten quid's fine.' He dug a note from his pocket and held it out.

'It's a size ten, too...' The woman's expression became doubtful. What was the matter with her, didn't she want to sell the fucking dress?

'Perfect.'

She took the ten pound note and smoothed it beneath her fingers on the counter.

'Right then. Hang on while I get it down.'

Jasper positioned himself behind the screen while she fiddled about on the other side.

After ages she stepped down, and laid the dress with a flourish along the counter. Of course there were other customers in here now, and she seemed hell-bent on making his purchase as conspicuous as possible, it was worse than buying johnnies. She faffed about with tissue paper, folding the dress over twice, smoothing it and tweaking it, until finally, at last she slipped it into a carrier bag and handed it to him.

'There we go.'

'Cheers,' he muttered.

'Hope she likes it!'

For the second time, Jasper fled, this time without looking back.

★ ★ ★

The difficulties of concealing the invitation were as nothing to those of concealing the red dress. On his return, both his parents' cars were in the drive, and as he approached the house the front door opened and Dobbo appeared.

'There he is,' cried his mother, at Dobbo's shoulder. 'Good timing. Stephen was looking for you.'

'Hi,' said Dobbo.

'Hi.'

'I'll leave you to it,' said Jasper's mother, leaving them on the doorstep.

'Where've you been?' Dobbo glanced at the carrier bag which Jasper had folded over and was carrying under his arm. 'Shopping?'

'Present,' said Jasper.

'Who for?'

In a moment of inspiration Jasper put his finger to his lips and nodded in the direction his mother had gone.

Dobbo nodded back. 'Got it. Fancy a kick around?'

'Not just now,' said Jasper. 'I've got stuff to do.'

'Right ... Going to Megan's party tonight?'

'Don't know.'

'Rachel's going.'

'I've got extra shifts.'

'Oh well,' said Dobbo, with ponderous sarcasm. 'I'd hate to come between a man and his work.'

'I need the money.'

'Yeah, well ... At least you're not revising.'

'Want to come in?' asked Jasper, none too warmly. He felt a bit of a shit saying no to everything, but all he wanted to do was get behind a locked door and test out the dress, which was burning a hole in his armpit.

To his colossal relief, Dobbo shook his head. 'I'm going to the rec.'

'Seeya.'

'Have fun.'

'Piss off.'

Dobbo took a few steps backwards, hands in pockets. 'I'll say hi to Rachel for you, yeah?'

'Don't bother.'

'I might anyway ... see how I feel.'

'You dare.'

'It's a free country.'

'Hands off, Dobbin. You never know, I might get there.'

Dobbo's face was a mask of scepticism. 'Sure.'

As Jasper closed the front door his mother stuck her head out of the kitchen. 'Stephen not coming in?'

'He's going down the rec for a kick-around.'

'Are you going?'

'Don't feel like it.'

He headed for the stairs, but he could feel her watching him. 'Jass—'

'What?'

'Are you okay? I mean, is everything all right?'

'Of course it is. Why wouldn't it be?'

She shrugged. 'I just wondered ... Exams coming up and everything. Don't work too hard.'

'I won't.'

'And the supermarket – your dad and I think you should pack that in until after GCSEs. It's too much. You'd be better off seeing your friends when you're not revising, having some fun. All work and no play—'

'I'm fine!'

He rarely raised his voice to his mother and instantly regretted it. She said gently: 'Just as long as you are.'

'I am, Mum.'

'But remember about the job, please, Jass.'

'I will.' He could feel his jaw tightening, his teeth clenching.

She looked at him for a second, with a soft, closed smile. A smile that said that her antennae were waving, but she wasn't going to pry, or take it any further. Then she turned back into the kitchen, and he went up the stairs and into his room.

One thing about that exchange, though he hadn't enjoyed it – he'd be left in peace till lunch. Not that he wasn't usually, but his mother would be extra careful to allow him his space and privacy now.

He went first to the bathroom and locked the door. He ripped his clothes off, including his boxers, and wriggled into the dress. There wasn't a long mirror in here, but he could tell just by the way the dress felt that it fitted perfectly, except for the top which he'd have to pad out – he'd need a strapless bra and some socks to put inside it. The fabulous colour suited his dark hair and pale skin, he looked sexy, glamorous, exotic – a woman with a past, not a callow, goal-scoring youth. He stood on tip-toe to get a better look and the movement reminded him of something else he was going to need – shoes! Hours earlier the bra and shoes issue would have done his head in, he'd have been freaking out with fear and frustration but now, wearing the red dress in all its flaming, OTT glory, he could have walked straight through the wall of Topshop, flung out his arms and announced, 'I want shoes and a bra – you got a problem with that?'

How he was going to walk in the shoes was another matter. He'd have to cross that bridge – in high heels – when he came to it.

He put the carrier bag containing the dress (which he rolled, the way he'd seen his mother do) in the outer-pocket of his suitcase, the one his dad had got him for the school skiing trip last year, and slung it back on the top of the wardrobe.

That afternoon, to keep everyone happy, he watched the Five Nations play-off with his father, which ended in a favourable result in more ways than one, because his father offered to run him into work. Jasper decided to try his luck.

'Dad – I might go to a party afterwards. Any chance of a lift home?'

'We're in, so I suppose – what time?'

'Not later than midnight ... I could give you a ring.'

'I don't see why not. Whereabouts is this party?'

'Megan's. The Walkers, those new houses in Hetheridge, you picked me up from that barbecue once.'

'I remember. All right, give us a ring in good time, though.'

'Cheers, Dad.'

'Hang on— ' Jasper's father leaned across as he closed the car door – 'how are you getting there?'

'I'll manage.'

'Let me know if you're stuck.'

'Will do.'

'And – hey, Jasper—'

'What?'

'Tell them you're not available for the next few weeks, right? It's important.'

'Okay.'

In spite of what had obviously been a genuine offer, he didn't want to test his father's goodwill any further than necessary, so during his tea break he called Micky.

'Yeah,' said Micky, in answer to his query about lifts, 'My sister, she won't mind.'

'You sure?'

'Sure I'm sure. What time do you finish?'

'Nine.'

'We'll pick you up at the car park entrance at nine.'

'Five past.'

'Whatever. We'll wait.'

Jasper arrived at the party demob happy having handed in his notice. He was glad he'd gone, because Rachel, who was a bit pissed, was extravagantly pleased to see him, and was also looking fantastic in a fuck-off black dress with a thin gold scarf tied round her hips like a belt. He glanced down at her shoes, which seemed to be nothing more than a vertical heel and two thin strands of diamante.

'Wicked shoes.'

'Like them?' She kicked a leg up sideways and waggled her foot. 'They're killing me but they're worth it.

Later, when they were snogging their way through 'Angels', she slipped them off and kicked them away, and at once sank down to her normal height, her breasts pressing against his solar plexus.

'That's better...'

Her mouth was so soft and wine-tasting, and her body so soft, yet springy in his arms that he could scarcely think of anything else. But when he tore himself away to go to the toilet he saw the shoes lying near the door and scooped one up. Inside the toilet he tried one on – or tried to, his toes barely went under the first strap, and they felt so high he couldn't imagine how anyone managed to move in them.

'Hey – wanker – for fuck's sake finish off in there!'

He left the shoe in the bathroom and opened the door. The lad outside barged past him and just made the toilet before barfing explosively. Jasper did hope none of it hit the shoe, because downstairs Rachel was looking for it.

'Who'd nick one shoe?' she asked, hopping about and grabbing his shoulder for support.

'A one-legged shoe fetishist?' he suggested. That made her laugh. And even better was that a bit later he went and rescued the shoe from the rank-smelling bathroom, and produced it with a flourish.

'This it?'

'Jass!' She kissed him, open-mouthed and moist. 'You're brilliant!'

'I know,' he said modestly.

Spring into Summer was only a few days away now. The countdown had begun, but the time between each tick yawned ever longer.

In the end he'd got some gold shoes, and a bra – ready stuffed! – from a costume-hire place. He'd had to throw in a bubble wig and a boa just to beef up the fancy dress story, but the hire of the whole lot together had come to scarcely more than he'd have to pay in a charity shop, so no complaints. On the Thursday, when his parents were out for a curry with friends, he tried on everything together, and it looked the biz. He was letting his hair grow on the pretext that it was bad luck to get it cut before exams, and it was so long that at school he had to wear it in a pony tail. There was a certain amount of ribbing from Dobbo and Micky about when the goatee was going to appear, but when he saw the overall effect there was no doubt it was worth it. He wasn't shaving yet, and there was only the merest hint of dark down on his upper lip, which he considered rather sexy.

There'd been no difficulty, either, with his pre-seeded excuse. When he mentioned it casually, his father said: 'Oh yes, how is he? Still suffering social hell in Bury St Edmunds?'

'Pretty much. So okay if I go up there on Saturday?'

'What about the fare?'

'I've got it.'

'Fine. Give us a ring if you need to get back from the station later on.'

'Might spend the night.'

'Let us know if you do,' said his mother.

'I will.'

The 'stay the night' thing was just to cover his taking a rucksack; he wouldn't be staying, because his was only a day-booking. For arrival and departure he was going to wear a pair of black trousers and a pale green scoop-neck T-shirt, another charity shop purchase. The black trousers weren't gender specific, the T-shirt he covered up with a grey Redsox hoodie. The dress and etceteras were for the evening reception: 'Drinks in the Orangery' was how it was billed, though what an Orangery was he hadn't the faintest. And he'd have to leave at eight to have the slightest chance of catching the last train.

On the morning itself he set off to walk to the station, but he felt so light, and full of energy, he could have run every step, rucksack or no rucksack. For the first time he had a real, personal understanding of something old Ma Mumford had taught them in Citizenship: that in a civilized country freedom and safety were the same thing.

For this one day, he was free to be himself – and would be perfectly safe.

Well, it was all right, but they were mostly old. Or older, anyway. He should have foreseen that. He'd sort of known, but the reality – middle-aged blokes in frocks (quite dull frocks, he was surprised to see) – was both comic and slightly depressing. Everyone had to have a 'dressed' name – a name they were known by when they were in women's clothes; he chose Gina, as being vaguely Italian and glamorous, but there were any number of Brendas, Daphnes and

Alisons, as if the people concerned wanted to look like respectable housewives or teachers or something. Hair was neat, jewellery discreet, make-up soft and natural ... where was the fun in that? Though Jasper could see that if you were going to go out and about in women's clothes, especially in a rural area like his, you were probably well-advised not to do the full lady-boy monty, even if you had the looks. Which most of these blokes didn't. It was the feel of womanliness they liked, the mixture of softness and restraint, the girl-talk and pampering.

Jasper didn't go much on the pampering, and he had no money to shop. He was picked out of the audience to be the hairdresser's model, so he got a free wash and blow dry, and having cottoned on to this he wangled a free make-up as well.

'Of course Gina has nice firm, young skin,' said the beautician, her little light, soft hands patting and stroking foundation on to his face. 'But the technique I'm going to show you works for all skin types...'

The difference between that and his own clumsy efforts at home was incredible. His face seemed to shine as if something had been lit inside, rather than merely applied to the surface. Several of the others came up to him afterwards and admired the beautician's handiwork.

'It's eyes I have a problem with,' said Jean. 'I don't have a steady enough hand.'

'Try doing it before you go to the pub,' said Hilary.

When the hilarity died down Jean said ruefully: 'But face it, whatever we do we're not going to look as good as Gina.'

The hair was another thing because of course most of them had to wear wigs. They were very good wigs, not like the ones in the costume-hire shop, but they still couldn't compete with the real thing. Soon, Jasper was walking tall.

There was unlimited tea, coffee and soft drinks, and at lunchtime he had to hold back from stuffing himself stupid from the stupendous buffet because he was worried he might not be able to do the dress up.

Perhaps because of the general lack of glamour, he wasn't shy with the others. Men whom he'd never have spoken to in other circumstances were chatty and friendly, there was a real sense of camaraderie to which he responded. At teatime he went out into the garden; a group were doing T'ai Chi and beckoned him to join in. In no time at all he was performing the slow, graceful movements, not feeling in the least self-conscious and rather enjoying the peace. When the sequence ended he sat down with his back against a tree and one of the others joined him.

'Is this your first time at one of these weekends?'

'Yes.'

'Enjoying it?'

'Yes,' said Jasper truthfully, 'it's great.'

'Donna, by the way.'

'Gina.'

Jasper submitted to a crunching handshake. It was surreal, but in a good way.

The time for the cocktail party approached. Most of the guests retreated to their rooms to change, but Jasper had devised a plan. The Gents and the Ladies in the Grantchester Suite were given over to the Spring into Summer contingent, so at five thirty he bagged the disabled cubicle which was big, with its own wash basin and a large mirror. Because he'd never gone dressed in public before, the element of display was important to him. And all the compliments had boosted his ego and his confidence: he wanted to turn heads, to be told he looked the best – not hard in this company, he suspected, but never mind.

The Orangery, he'd discovered, was a sort of long conservatory running down the side of the hotel, overlooking the lawn where they'd done the T'ai Chi. It was some distance from the ladies' cloakroom, so it was impossible to hear when the party was underway, he had to guess, and anyway he had to strike a happy medium between making an entrance and allowing enough time before changing back for the train home.

At six fifteen he repacked his rucksack and emerged. He felt a million dollars, and the mirror in there told him he looked it. The only thing he was having a bit of trouble with was the shoes, he had to plant each foot with great care and deliberation to avoid spraining an ankle, but at least this resulted in what he hoped was a sort of catwalk stalk.

When he went to return his rucksack to reception, he saw the look of admiration on the girl's face long before he got there. When he handed over the rucksack, she said: 'It'll be in the back there, if you need anything.' Then she added, in a quite different voice: 'That's a fantastic dress.'

'Like it?' He glanced down at himself, one hand smoothing the gleaming, scarlet satin. He was wearing a jock strap but the bulge still showed a little, and he was proud of it.

'Mmm ... You look really lovely.'

'Thanks.'

'The party's through there.' She pointed, and he felt her eyes on him as he walked away, praying he wouldn't stumble or do anything else stupid to ruin the effect.

There were already about thirty people in the Orangery. Because it was a beautiful evening they'd opened the doors and some were outside on the terrace. Near the door was a long white-clothed table with champagne, orange juice and bottles of sparkling water. Other tables were dotted around here and there with little dishes of olives and cashew nuts, but no one was sitting down. Jasper took a buck's fizz – the waitress called him 'madam' which was both weird and exciting. Several people looked round at him and one of them even clapped, a group opened to receive him.

'Gina...!' It was Donna, his friend from the garden. 'Will you look at this! Might have known you'd steal the show!'

There was a general chorus of agreement and admiration. Donna asked where he'd found the dress.

'I can't believe you got that in a charity shop! What sort of people live in your area?'

'It was a one-off. They had it in the window.'

'I bet they did. Bloody hell, it might have

been made for you.'

'It is hand-made,' said Jasper, enjoying himself. 'They told me.'

'Jammy or what?' complained Jean, affably. 'All they've got in our Oxfam is musty crimplene and horrible unlined slacks with elasticated waists.'

'Don't knock elasticated,' said Hilary, 'not all of us are sylphlike. I don't know where I'd be without it.'

'Anyway,' said Donna. 'Here's to Gina, for showing us what can be done.'

'Gina!' They all raised their glasses. Jasper thought he must have died and gone to heaven.

'Hang on though,' said Donna. 'Here comes the competition.'

They all looked towards the door. A tall figure in a long black dress had just come in and was standing, glass of champagne in hand, surveying the room as if she owned it.

'Lois!' called Hilary. 'Lois – over here.'

The tall figure sashayed over.

'Lois,' said Hilary. 'Great frock by the way – meet Gina.'

There was mischief in the air at the sight of the two best-dressed people in the room coming face to face. But no one, not in a zillion years, could have guessed the full extent of the mischief.

'Hallo, Gina,' said Lois, without batting an eyelid. 'That is a wonderful outfit.'

'So's yours,' said Jasper in a steady voice, gazing back into the frosty grey eyes of Mr Mather. 'Good choice. Black's always cool.'

Jasper stayed for another half an hour, but they didn't speak to each other after that. Not for any particular reason, it was just easier not to. From time to time Jasper would glance around to see where Mr Mather was, and spot the tall, elegant black figure in another part of the room, and his whole chest would fill with huge shiny bubbles of amusement, astonishment and delight.

Result!

It wasn't that he wished Mr Mather any ill, far from it. His secret was safe with Jasper, and Jasper was pretty sure it was mutual. But if he needed one final endorsement, one big sign that said IT'S OKAY TO WEAR WOMEN'S CLOTHES, this was it!

At six forty-five Jasper said good-bye to his new friends (on the clear understanding that if they were ever, any time or anywhere, to meet each other on the street they'd walk straight past) and headed first to reception for his rucksack, then to the ladies to change. Only one of the cubicles was occupied, and as he walked in the toilet flushed and out came Mr Mather, still tweaking the hem of his dress.

'Oh,' he said. 'Hallo Gina.'

'Hallo, sir,' said Jasper, from habit, now it was just the two of them.

'Enjoying the weekend?' asked Mr Mather, rotating his hands under the dryer.

'I'm just going, actually,' said Jasper.

'Are you?' Mr Mather turned round, still shaking his hands, trying to keep the relief out of his voice.

'Yeah, got to get home.'

'Revision, I suppose...'

'That's right...'

Jasper had his hand on the disabled door, and Mather was at the exit, when Mather said: 'Oh – by the way.'

Jasper paused. He was so fucking calm, it was mad.

'You realize – well, I'm sure you do but no harm in reminding you as it's your first time – you realize there's a protocol—'

'A what?'

'A way of doing things. The whole point of these weekends is that they're private—'

'I know—'

'Confidential, I suppose, is the word. Yes, confidential. Everything here is strictly confidential.'

'Yes, I—'

'So obviously, as far as you and I are concerned—'

'Sir!' Jasper rapped it out, he knew that'd make Mr Mather pay attention, and he did, looking a bit startled and green about the gills beneath his concealing mousse and sunglow blusher. 'Yes, sir,' said Jasper gently. 'Don't worry. I understand.'

Fifteen minutes later Jasper set off, bidding a cheery farewell to the receptionist and heading down the drive. He was too early for the courtesy bus, but he'd allowed an hour to walk to the station, which was more than enough. It was a perfect evening, the sky a fading duck-egg blue, the fields lush and green, with the occasional blanket of brilliant yellow, sweet-smelling rape, the hedges boiling over with cow-parsley, blackthorn and primroses.

Beyond one gateway was a meadow full of long grass and buttercups. The ears of a rabbit stuck up through the grass in the middle. Jasper climbed over the gate and waded through the grass, watching the rabbit zig-zag away from him. When he was in the centre of the field, about where the rabbit had originally been, he lay down, flat on his back, with his arms spread out, the way he'd used to make 'angels' in the snow with his mother when he was little. The fragrant grass sprang up round him, protectively. Above him a faint, dappled moon was just appearing in the still-sunlit sky.

Jasper stretched his fingers and toes to their very limit as he lay there. And laughed and laughed and laughed.

Maurice

If there was a type of actor Maurice found impossible to handle, it was the 'semi-pro'. He used the mental inverted commas because the appellation was emphatically not his, but theirs. 'Semi-professional' didn't feature in his lexicon. There were professionals – and then there were amateurs. (In Maurice's mind the ghostly prefix 'rank' hovered before the latter). On the other hand, give him 'real' amateurs any day, people without pretensions who were in it for 'the experience'.

Now that he was a hired gun, the kind of job he preferred (outside of legit, commercial theatre which was rapidly assuming the status of hen's teeth in his life) was the community production, where everyone who turned up on the day, irrespective of talent, looks, age or gender, got a part. You pitched your direction, and your ambitions, at the level of the youngest or least able (the two things were by no means synonymous) and everyone knew exactly where they were. The good ones flew, the not-so-good clung to their coat-tails, the completely palsied and useless faffed around happily in the background. But absolutely no one banged on about their motivation or their through-line. They stood on their marks and spoke their words.

Maurice had Hamlet's advice to the players laminated and pinned up on the back of his downstairs lavatory door. He quoted it often.

When a whole group called itself semi-professional it meant they had access to the civic theatre twice a year, and harboured at least one Nth-rater who had been in rep in the fifties. So it was that Diana, Maurice's agent, handed him the letter with a knowing look.

'Not your favourite, I realize that.'

'Jesus wept.'

'You did say you wanted something in September.'

'Yes, but I never said I was desperate.'

'I'm told it's a very nice town, and well within your commuting radius.'

'Oh, I bet it's nice.' Maurice tossed the letter down on Diana's desk. 'QED.'

'So that's a no, is it?'

'Yes. It's a no.' Diana picked up the letter.

'No – God, I don't know.'

Diana put the letter down again. 'You've done *Friday Fortnight* before?'

'I've no idea. It just feels as if I have, times without number.'

She glanced down. ' "...want to do justice to Marlon Sibowitz's dazzling farce" it says here.'

'Stop it ... Stop now!' cried Maurice.

' "...a small, keen, well-resourced group with ideas above our station..." '

'And a joker! There always has to be a joker.'

'Well-resourced,' mused Diana, removing her glasses. 'What can we infer from that?'

'That they're a bunch of blazered oafs and ladies who lunch, who've taken up drama for its unrivalled extra-curricular shagging opportunities.'

'Probably,' agreed Diana, twiddling the glasses thoughtfully. 'But also that we may be able to push them a little on the fee...'

The audition was on a Sunday evening towards the end of July. This, he was advised via email by the Chairman of the Pear Tree Players, was because then the cast could go away and learn their lines during August, when rehearsals were out of the question.

Maurice had heard all this before and considered it shite. In his experience, amateur actors learnt fuck-all while browsing and sluicing their way through Tuscany, or Provence, or wherever, and would turn up for blocking in early September in that irritating state of half-knowing, or pretending to know, their lines, with one hand still surgically attached to the book. If he'd had his way, auditions would have been set for the middle of August, with a first read-through and blocking taking place immediately and twice-weekly rehearsals following on thereafter: books down at week three, non-negotiable.

But never mind, he told himself. Diana had been right about the fee, and he himself took a grim, masochistic pleasure in having his worst suspicions concerning this job confirmed at an early stage. It was all going to be exactly as he'd feared and predicted, but he would see it through. He, after all, was a professional, it was why they'd hired him.

The audition was in the Players' rehearsal room, a small modern hall semi-attached to a Methodist chapel. At least there was a car park, and as Maurice pulled in, a man in jeans and a linen jacket was unlocking the door. It seemed to be quite a performance, and not wanting to intrude on private grief Maurice remained in the car. When the door eventually yielded, the man turned round, and gave a half-wave, then saw who it probably was, and waved more enthusiastically. He began walking towards the car and Maurice got out.

'Can it be Maurice?'

'That's right, Maurice Wolfe.'

'I'm Colin Coleman, Players' chairman, absolutely delighted.'

'Nice to meet you,' said Maurice, thinking, if ever there was a formulaic response, that was it.

'No trouble getting here?' asked Coleman, leading the way to the hall.

'None at all, thanks to the wonders of the internet.'

'Come along in. I apologize for not being here already.'

'But you were,' said Maurice, allowing himself a little gentle sarcasm.

'I mean inside, door open, chairs set out, ready for business.'

'I was early.'

'That's true.' Coleman pointed a finger at him like a gun. 'Still, perhaps it's all to the good that you're here as people come in – not being confronted with that sea of hopeful anonymous faces.'

'I'm used to it.'

'Of course you are ... Now, look,' said Coleman, suddenly brisk. 'I'm going to get the place ready, put the kettle on —'

'Do what?'

'Put the kettle on.'

'What for?'

'Tea, coffee, get things off on a sociable footing.'

'But,' pointed out Maurice, 'it's not a social occasion.'

'Not social, no, but no reason why it shouldn't be sociable.' Coleman made the distinction with slightly pointed politeness. 'We find a cuppa at the outset helps to oil the wheels. Look, Maurice – have a wander, familiarize yourself, while I do those things etcetera...'

He strode off into the kitchen and Maurice heard water rattling busily into a kettle. Obediently, he wandered, though there wasn't a lot to see. The room was high-ceilinged, beige-carpeted, magnolia throughout. There were long stacking tables of the sort to be found in all such premises, and piles of chairs ditto. In one corner was a Yamaha organ, and next to it a different sort of table with a clutter of objects – sheet music, nightlights in jam-jars, a small folding lectern, a pile of books, a vase of artificial flowers and a wooden crucifix.

Coleman came back in and began setting out chairs in a semi-circle. 'They have services in here, sometimes. And other functions. They're not our flavour, but I believe they're well liked.'

'Good,' said Maurice, not knowing what else to say.

'They were certainly a godsend to us,' said Coleman, dragging a table into the centre to face the chairs. 'Before this we were in the scout hut, and it was absolutely perishing.'

Maurice remembered 'well-resourced', but decided not to mention it. After all, they had very properly decided to spend their funds on a professional director, so who was he to complain?

'Okay. Cups, cups...'

Coleman disappeared into the kitchen again. Maurice dropped his copy of the play on the table, and sat down. He opened the book and, head in hand, pencil between his fingers, began to read. One might as well be discovered in an appropriate attitude. A moment later there was the sound of a car outside, and another, followed by the slamming of doors, greetings, and voices approaching the hall. He was careful not to look up until the people were actually inside and someone, a woman, said: 'Mr Wolfe?'

Now he lifted his head and treated the new arrivals to his famous heavy lidded, slightly distracted, fiercely intelligent stare. The woman, completely unfazed, bore down on him with her hand extended. She was fiftyish and had once been told she was fascinating. She may once even have been fascinating, but now she was over-presented and over-projecting to such an extent that he wondered whether she might be the pretext for the 'semi-professional' tag in Coleman's letter.

She introduced herself as Alice Wing, and then presented the others, Dennis Blacker and Audrey Sammes. Dennis was the youngest there, might have been late thirties on a good day with the light behind him; Audrey was grand and smart and probably looked younger than she was.

Colin came through from the kitchen.

'Right, orders taken here. Maurice, what will you have?'

What Maurice would have liked at that moment was his hip flask, but he said: 'Just a glass of water thanks.'

'Water it is, and you lot? Think I know...'

Dennis and Audrey gravitated to the kitchen to fetch the drinks and Alice sat down in the centre of the row of chairs and fished *Friday Fortnight* out of a capacious burgundy corduroy bag.

'I can't begin to tell you,' she said, 'how knocked out we are to have you.'

Maurice managed a slightly chilly smile. 'Well ... Let's hope we can crack this,' he said, tapping his copy.

'Can't wait,' said Alice.

Another three people arrived, again two women and one man – the usual ratio – Don, Janice and Marian. All were forty-somethings, and while not actually hideous, were certainly not glamorous. *Friday Fort-night* had a cast of seven, including one newly married couple, a lothario, and that old-fashioned thing, a femme fatale. Maurice sighed inwardly. There was another round of handshaking, more orders taken for tea.

By the time they were all sitting down, teacups on the floor, books on laps, there were nine auditioners, of whom Dennis was by far the youngest. But Dennis had an overbite, a prominent adam's apple, and a carrier bag.

'Right,' said Maurice. 'Shall we begin?'

There was a murmur of assent, their eyes were upon him. In spite of everything he experienced a frisson of pleasure at his own power and status. Diana had told him to think of this as a challenge, but by God, he was the man who had brought Beckett to the Borough Theatre, Coddling St Thomas, and made it pay! Alongside that, an amusing if predictable modern farce in this town, with these people, should be a stroll in the park. Maurice wheeled out the charm, turning his book face down and treating the Pear Tree Players to his special dark, confiding, rather wicked smile as a prelude to his party trick.

'Just before we do,' he said, 'let me check that I have your names right.'

He did, of course, moving from left to right, making eye contact and saying each person's name as he went. He claimed no virtue or skill, it was a gift he had, which had stood him in good stead over the years. And now it worked again. The smiles followed his progress like a Mexican wave. They were enchanted, and even gave him a little round of applause.

'And I'm Maurice,' he said, 'so now we're all best friends.'

This got a laugh. He saw Alice and Colin glance at each other in a moment of happy collusion, their judgement vindicated.

'I'm going to spend five minutes,' he continued, 'letting you know where I'm coming from, and what will inform my casting of this very funny play.'

Their expressions became serious, reflecting his tone of voice, brows drew together in concentration, copies of *Friday Fortnight* were clasped like talismans in both hands, tongues slid expectantly over lips.

'...joking, of course, I don't know you, I've got no agenda but the play, and that's why you've asked me here. To be dispassionate, to help you be the best that you can be.'

Always a popular line. Pure flannel of course, but you couldn't go wrong with a spot of touchy-feely these days. He could practically hear that cheesy song about searching for a hero inside yourself playing in their heads. Once more unto the breach ... we few, we happy few ... for he today...

'...not necessarily looking for the obvious people. I don't typecast. Casting against the role can yield really exciting results, so I hope none of you are harbouring fixed ideas about who's most suitable for what part. I'll be the judge of that – I'm a benign dictator!'

This met with another round of laughter, rather nervous this time. That was good. They had to trust him, but they had to be shaken up, too, like a bunch of raw recruits learning to toe the line.

'It goes without saying that right through the rehearsal period, up until production week, I'll always listen to any ideas you may have, but the final decision rests with me. I hope that's Okay.' He lowered his eyes as he said these last words, they were framed as a query but presented as an ultimatum. Their murmured agreement was like an 'Amen'.

'Right,' he said. 'Let's read Act One, Scene Three. Alice take Julia, Dennis read David and Audrey, would you be Helen. Away we go.'

He wound up the proceedings at eight thirty, having heard all he needed to. Whatever the pretensions or aspirations of the Pear Tree Players, they were a fairly standard lot. And whatever his brave words earlier, this audition could never be a completely level playing field. Everyone here was going to get a part, bar one – and the brutal truth was that unless he took it upon himself to rewrite vast tracts of Marlon Sibowitz's text, the parts they got would be largely determined by age.

He was now convinced that Alice had had some professional training or experience; she was by far the best reader, but that often meant less room for improvement. Dennis, though something of a stumbler, had a sense of comedy which meant he might be able to play the young married man, with references to romantic good looks and athleticism soft-pedalled. Colin wasn't bad – he had the sort of nondescript but unexceptionable appearance which could play up or down, and he had read pretty well: a useful all-rounder. The elderly lady, Audrey, had read fluently but without the smallest attempt at characterization – her Julia LeVay was indistinguishable from her Ethel Flannery. But maybe that would come.

It was left that he would email his cast-list to Colin within the next couple of days, and they'd re-convene at the same time and place for a read-through in one week's time, before scattering to the four winds for the whole of August.

He sat and made notes while the hall was cleared, and then accompanied Colin out into the car park.

'Do you know,' said Colin, 'I have a good feeling about this play.'

'Really?' Maurice had been unable to keep the surprise out of his voice, and added more emolliently: 'Farce is hard work, but everyone seems to have good attitude.'

'They do, they really do...' Colin shook his head in a kind of wonderment. 'And it's all down to you.'

'Let's see,' said Maurice, with a dry laugh. 'I haven't done anything yet.'

Colin wished him a safe journey, and

zoomed off in his MG. Maurice took a moment to enjoy the blessed privacy of his car, removing his jacket, lighting a cigarette and choosing a CD for the homeward journey. He was just about to turn the key in the ignition, when the car park was briefly flooded by headlights and a sleek Jaguar pulled up next to him, on the right. The driver got out, paused, seemed to experience a moment's indecision and then peered in his direction. There was no denying the late arrival of a stray Pear Tree Player.

Unwillingly, nay, grumpily, virtually grinding his teeth, Maurice clambered out.

'Can I help?' he asked.

'Oh – no, I have a horrible feeling I've missed it altogether. The audition?'

'I'm afraid you have.'

'How infuriating. I thought I might make it for the last fifteen minutes or so and creep in as third rustic on the left or something.'

Maurice laughed. It was the first genuine laugh, the happiest, the most pleasure he'd experienced all evening. And why wouldn't it be, when he was talking to the most beautiful woman he'd ever seen?

'Don't worry,' he said. 'It's not cast yet.'

'No, but I wasn't there to read, and this outside dir—' She stopped and pulled a little apologetic face. 'Just a second, that's not you, by any chance?'

'Actually, yes. Maurice Wolfe, how do you do?'

'Oh, dear...' She closed her eyes, touched a hand to her brow, then held it out to him. 'Carolyn Summerby. And I am never usually late. Ask anyone.' She looked around the empty car park, and laughed. 'Really!'

'I'm sure.'

'Still, there we are. Naturally I don't expect a part after turning up late first time out, it's too shaming. I shall see if I can make myself useful back stage. Or front of house.'

'That seems an awful waste.' He'd said the words at the same time as thinking them, but her own embarrassment seemed to prevent her noticing his.

'No, no, poor timekeeping would rule out anyone in my book.'

'But you don't usually keep poor time.' He brushed aside her demur. 'You said so. And I believe you.'

'Well, you're being more than civil, but it's academic anyway, because I didn't read for a part.'

It was one of those rare occasions when his status was a social asset. He began to move away, but said over his shoulder:

'Come to the read-through this time next week, and let's see what happens.'

'All right,' she said. 'Thank you. I will. And I shall be here first.'

He drove the first mile on autopilot, unable to think of anything but her. Caroline ... no – Carolyn. Maurice – thrice married but more often, as now, single – had met many attractive women in his time. Most actresses were good looking, very often strikingly so. It had been gratifying to discover, over time, that he was not unattractive himself. But tonight for the first time in the presence of true beauty, he had been humbled.

She'd been like a lovely distrait dryad, standing there in the half-light in some kind of long, loose tunic and trousers, with her exquisite pale face, its frail, sculpted jaw and cheekbones, the hair like silvery feathers, wide, shadowed, faunlike eyes, the long, slender neck and fragile shoulders ... She'd been so thin as to be almost transparent but Maurice – who usually considered himself a meat-and-potatoes man – had been overwhelmed by that thinness, it was almost as if he could see her soul flickering inside her, and that was beautiful too. Like a flame burning inside a tall glass lamp. He couldn't remember when he'd last been so intoxicated by another person.

He was shocked to discover that he was now on the motorway and could scarcely remember how he'd got there. What's more the speedometer showed that he was travelling at over a hundred. He broke out in a sweat as he slowed and shifted back across the lanes to the inside and a safer, duller pace and position. When he saw a sign for services he pulled over, and bought himself a disgusting cappuccino, all froth and no flavour, in the café. Sitting at a table by the window, watching the lights on the south-bound carriageway whiz past, Maurice realized that he couldn't possibly let her go. He had the power to keep her, and by God, he would.

Carolyn Summerby didn't haunt his dreams as he'd expected she might, for the simple reason that he lay awake for so long thinking about her that when he did drop off it was into the sleep of the dead. Then of course he awoke late, and disorientated, to the sound of the phone. He stumbled, cursing, out of bed and down the stairs, and picked it up just as his own voice cut in with the recorded message.

Hi, not able to answer right now but leave your—

'Hallo?'

'Maurice, it's me.'

'Diana ... What time is it?'

'Oh – nine thirty?'

'Holy shit.'

'I'm so sorry, did I disturb you?'

'I've overslept, bugger.'

'Would you like me to call back later?'

'No, no, I'm here now,' he growled un-graciously, grappling one-handed with the tie of his happy coat, 'and I should be up anyway.'

'I couldn't possibly comment,' said Diana. She could be an arsey cow in her quiet way, what business was it of hers what time he got out of bed?

'What can I do for you?' he asked.

'It's more a case of what I can do for you.'

'Are you going to tell me or not?'

'Look, Maurice—' There was a brief, irrit-able pause. He pictured Diana taking her glasses off and pinching the skin between her brows. 'We seem to have got off on the wrong foot. Why don't I call back later.'

'No!' Maurice was suddenly swept by the memory of Carolyn Summerby, her beauty and sweetness, the unforced gracefulness of her manners. In other words, he was asham-ed, and it was a new experience for him.

'Sorry. You know what it's like when you

oversleep.'

'The best form of defence is attack.'

'Something like that.'

'Okay. To cut to the chase, I had Charlie Fetters on the phone at close of play last night.'

Fetters was a producer, a little younger than Maurice, who in the view of those whose opinion Maurice solicited had gone a long way on remarkably little talent. The phrase 'Midas touch' had frequently been attached to his name in the press.

'Oh yes?'

'I know you're not his greatest fan—'

'Correct.'

'And he's not my favourite person either, but listen. He's putting together a show, and he wants you to be in it.'

'In it?'

'That's right. It's—'

'But I don't do "in it", do I? Or not for donkey's years. What's he on about?'

'Maurice, listen!'

'I beg your pardon.'

'It's a kind of review about the theatre, to run from the third week of August to end of September in Brighton. The idea is that there will be five of you – a playwright, two actors, a director and an impresario – talking and telling anecdotes. Working title *The*

Play's the Thing.'

'It sounds ghastly,' said Maurice, flattered in spite of himself. 'Aren't we all going to sound appallingly up our own arses?'

'Probably, but that won't matter. The Little Theatre's available and it's a wonderful low-effort way to fill it with a crowd-pleaser for the summer.'

'But I can't, anyway,' said Maurice. 'I've got the Pear Tree Players.'

'I'll come to that. Do you want to know who else is interested so far?' She rattled off some names, all people he'd heard of and respected. 'You'd be in good company.'

'I don't know ... He's such a prat.'

'A prat with a fat budget and an address book to die for.'

'And it would mean dropping the Pear Trees in the shit.'

'Actually, no,' said Diana. 'I took the liberty of phoning Nigel Staines, and he's willing and able to step into your shoes if need be.'

Maurice closed his eyes. The moment he did so he saw Carolyn in all her loveliness, shining like a nymph in that car park.

'Maurice?'

'Yup, still here.'

'I wouldn't normally suggest you switch like this, but the timing's not fatal, not if you make the break immediately, and Nigel takes over. This really is a super opportunity, you know how much you'd enjoy it and I know how brilliant you'd be. It's exactly the sort of production that could take on a life of its own, be put on all over the place at a moment's notice for years to come. Think of that, I could probably sort you out with a slice! Plus, the money's good and it would almost certainly lead to other things.' She paused, and when he didn't answer, added: 'Rather more challenging and interesting things than the Pear Tree Players.'

He knew she was right, but the habit of touchiness died hard.

'Not so long ago you were selling them to me like a street Arab.'

'Yes,' said Diana, 'but that was then. I'm a pragmatist.'

Maurice closed his eyes again, and Carolyn Summerby was still there.

'May I think about it?'

'For about five minutes.'

'You're all heart, aren't you?'

'It's for your own good, Maurice. And also, obviously, Charlie's keen to get the whole thing together by the day before yesterday.'

'I'll call back by lunchtime. If he wants me that much he can wait till then.'

'All right. Call it midday.'

'Call it what you like.' He caught himself again and said: 'Thanks, Diana.'

'I aim to please.'

In fact it took him less than five minutes to make up his mind. This was, if not a once-in-a-lifetime opportunity, at least a good one, with numerous intriguing possibilities. He was at the stage in his career when he needed a new direction, an opening-up, and though he'd spent the last fifteen years on the other side of the lights, Diana had placed an unerring finger on his exhibition-ist tendencies...

'Diana?'

'Golly, that was quick.'

'Yes, well, I can be quick when I want to.'

'Excellent. And?'

'I'll have to say no.'

'No!'

'Yes.'

'I mean no, you can't!'

Maurice closed his eyes for support and inspiration, which he duly received.

'I can't possibly let them down. It would be inexcusable.'

'Maurice...! You wouldn't be letting any-one down, you've barely cast the damn play and Nigel's like a greyhound in the slips waiting to take over.'

'Put him back in the kennel then.'

'I don't get it. Whence all these scruples all of a sudden?'

'Diana, I'm wounded.'

'You know what I mean.' She sighed heavily, he could picture the glasses, the frown-pinching, the lighting of a cigarette. 'Charlie's going to be disappointed.'

'That'll be a rare character-forming experience for him.'

'For good reasons, Maurice.'

'You know my views.'

'I don't like him much either, but he's a useful person to be in with.'

'Look, I'm sorry if I've saddled you with an awkward phone call—'

'It's not that—'

'But the answer's no. I'm not trying to insult him, for Christ's sake, it's perfectly straightforward, I'm already booked, okay?'

'OK.'

'Speak to you soon.'

'Right.'

He didn't like parting from Diana on this slightly sour note, but he knew it wouldn't last. He'd snapped out of it, so would she. They were like an old married couple who'd been together so long that they'd attained perfect symbiosis. And now that the decision was made, he felt wonderfully light-hearted.

The die had been cast, now it was the turn of the play. Showered, dressed and armed with treacly arabbica coffee, Maurice immersed himself in *Friday Fortnight*. With so little choice, it should have been simple, but there was no getting away from the fact that the available talent would stretch to six of the seven parts, but however he shuffled them there was always one which didn't quite fit. Not that it couldn't be done, but that it would not in his professional opinion, be done well. On the other hand Carolyn Summerby was coming to the reading, so perhaps all was not yet lost.

She was there first, as she'd promised, helping Colin set out the chairs. She'd swapped the graceful tunic and trousers for work-man-like jeans and loafers with a crisp white shirt, in which, if anything, she looked even more gorgeous.

'Hallo – you see? Good as my word.'

'I'm impressed.'

'Hi Maurice,' said Colin. 'Thanks for the cast list, I've disseminated it.'

'Everyone happy, I hope.'

'No question. Your word is law.'

'Glad to hear it. Then we can get stuck in.'

'Absolutely,' said Colin, 'and don't worry, we shan't bother with tea this evening, you'll want to hit the ground running.'

'I suggest we take five at the interval,' said Maurice. 'People could have one then if they want.'

'Good idea!'

'Us and our tea,' said Carolyn. 'What are we like?'

The popular slang phrase sounded charmingly out of place in her mouth, and he found himself smiling.

'I'm a slave to caffeine when I'm working at home.'

'Ah,' she said, not looking at him, tweaking a chair, 'but caffeine is cool.'

Maurice suspected he was being teased, but it was like being tickled with swansdown.

'I hadn't thought of it like that.'

He sat down at the table, and Colin placed a glass of water at his elbow. 'There you go ... And here they are.'

To give them their due, there wasn't even a hint of discord and, he noticed, they'd all highlighted their parts with marker pen. Except for Seamus and Carolyn who sat together, also uncomplaining, with pristine copies. Maurice had given considerable thought to how he would play this, and had concluded that it would be best dealt with straight away.

'Now it won't have escaped your attention,' he said, 'that we have more people here than there are in the cast. This is because I had an embarrass de richesse and so Seamus on this occasion did not get a part. And Carolyn arrived late, didn't you?' He and Carolyn shared a laugh. 'But was nevertheless inexplicably keen to be involved. So I suggested they both come along tonight to acquaint themselves with the play. What I would like,' he said seriously, addressing Seamus and Carolyn, 'is for the two of you to take turns on the book, and be general understudies.'

'Fine,' said Seamus. His accent was as thick and rich as a peat bog and Maurice could only pray that none of the male actors succumbed to illness.

'A perfect solution,' agreed Carolyn. She leaned towards Seamus, lucky man, and said in a lowered voice, 'You and I can compare diaries and work out which days nearer the time.'

Seamus ignored her, the bastard, looking up at Maurice and asking quite truculently: 'I take it you're not expecting us to learn the whole play?'

'Good grief, no. But by being on the book you'll become pretty familiar with it, and if someone does drop out you'll be surprised how much you do already know. Anyway, there's no shame in carrying a copy if necessary. Better that than a stumbling shambles, any day.'

Seamus nodded. 'Seems reasonable.'

Maurice hoped Seamus wasn't going to be trouble. There was something in his manner. Seems reasonable? What sort of comment was that from a bloody amateur? Of course it was fucking reasonable! Still, he noted, calming, Carolyn was sitting with downcast eyes, like a delightfully studious child, studying the first page.

'So.' Maurice opened his copy and pushed his chair back from the table so that he could rest his left leg on the opposite knee. 'I think we should go right through, stopping for no man, take a short break at the interval, and save any discussion for afterwards.'

The first half took just over an hour and wasn't bad. In fact Maurice could almost say he was pleasantly surprised. Everyone appeared to have studied their parts and even the less fluent ones, like Dennis, were having a real stab at characterization.

Audrey made a somewhat patrician Mrs Flannery; it might be possible to make a comedic virtue out of that – on the other hand one had strenuously to avoid over characterization, especially in the smaller parts. The determination to make a memorable cameo of what Carolyn had described as the 'third rustic on the left', resulting in flagrant and distracting upstaging, was an acknowledged tendency among amateurs: most of them would need calming down rather than geeing up.

'So far, so good,' he said, turning his open copy face-down on the table. 'Let's take a ten minute break.'

He declined a drink (though he'd have killed for a proper coffee), and went outside for a cigarette. He didn't want to get into discussion with anyone at this point, he needed to distance himself from the proceedings, and Carolyn in particular. She had followed the read-through with close attention, now and then smiling to herself, putting her finger to her mouth as if considering it, once or twice laughing out loud. There was a charming generosity of spirit about her, she enhanced the exercise just by being there. The contrast between Carolyn and Seamus, fidgeting and gurning in the seat next to her could not have been more marked. The temptation to say to her, 'You were wonderful' was overwhelming, and needed to be resisted.

'I hate to disturb your contemplative moment...'

'Not at all. Hallo.'

It was Alice (his femme fatale), this evening in a long dress with an asymmetric hem, and a necklace composed of what looked like animal teeth and stainless steel nuts. She held up a cigarette.

'My excuse for disturbing you.'

'We are the new lepers,' he agreed.

They took a companionable drag. He could sense a kind of suppressed overture of fidgeting and sure enough, a moment later she spoke.

'I realize you don't want to know the back story of everyone in the play.'

'Indeed I don't.'

'Quite. And believe me, I couldn't agree more. The play's the thing.'

Her cliché reminded him of what he had given up for this, and why, and he said brusquely: 'I sense a "but" approaching.'

'I do think you ought to know about Carolyn.'

He was sure he only hesitated for a nanosecond. 'Ought I?'

'You were so right to include her, she's

been through complete hell in the past year.'

'I'm sorry to hear that.' His heart pattered and stumbled and his hand, raising the cigarette to his lips, trembled. 'Let's hope this cheers her up.'

Alice was looking at him now, with a steady, challenging stare as if daring him to shirk his responsibilities. 'Her husband of twenty-five years left her. Cold. Walked out without even a clean handkerchief just after their silver wedding anniversary.'

'No,' said Maurice with as little feeling as he could manage. 'Bastard.'

'There'd been some chit of a girl young enough to be his daughter.'

'Chit of a girl.' There, thought Maurice, was an expression which used without irony, as now, was a sure indication that one was in the provinces. In fact it could have been one of the character descriptions in *Friday Fortnight* along with lothario and femme fatale...

'Ghastly,' he agreed absentmindedly.

'Yes, well, if one were being charitable one might blame the male menopause,' said Alice acidly. 'But what made it so much worse was that it transpired there'd been loads of others. He'd been playing away for years and no one knew, his antics made a complete mockery of twenty-five years of what she took to be happy marriage.'

Now Maurice was genuinely shocked.

'That's appalling!'

'Isn't it?'

'And she's so—' He regrouped. 'She's such a delightful woman.'

'Precisely. So you see—' Alice dropped her half-smoked cigarette and ground it out beneath her fringed boot – 'she needs all the morale-boosting she can get.'

'Point taken,' said Maurice, his breast seething with mixed emotions – pity, sorrow, chagrin for his whole sex, and wild jubilation. 'I'll definitely bear it in mind.'

'How's it going?' Colin leaned out of the door. 'We're all ready when you are.'

A couple of scenes from the end, Maurice held up his hand.

'I know I said no interruptions, but our understudies have been sitting here patiently all evening, and I think it's only right that they have a turn, particularly since I have yet to hear Carolyn read.' A general murmur of agreement greeted this announcement, and he continued: 'So I'd like Seamus, if you would, to read Miles, and Carolyn, perhaps you'd pick up Julia.'

From the corner of his eye he caught Alice's approving nod, but studiously avoided looking at her. The last thing he wanted was to be her co-conspirator in the Rehabilitation of Carolyn. Now he knew the score, he could do that all by himself.

Julia didn't reappear until the final scene, but the big rapprochement between Miles and Fiona pitched Seamus straight into the thick of it. Maurice kept his head down, following the lines in his book and trying to re-conceive nice, Oxbridge-educated home-counties Miles as a Guinness-guzzling bog-trotter with a charm bypass. At least Seamus had no problem with the pre-rapproch-ment confrontation. When Fiona shrieked: 'I thought you were the last gentleman alive, but you're a pig like all the rest!' you could see exactly what she meant. But the making-up was more problematic: billing and cooing simply weren't in Seamus's tool-box.

Still, there was nothing there that Maurice didn't know already. He found himself almost quivering with anticipation at the prospect of Carolyn's debut. Julia had some terrific lines in this final scene – witty, poignant, world-weary lines – and he could hardly wait to hear them delivered by this stunning and (as he now knew) damaged woman.

And then – she was terrible.

The disappointment was crushing. Maurice could have wept. For himself, for her, for the whole damn enterprise. As her small, flat, unprojected voice with no scintilla of expression or emotion, meandered along, he sat with his head down, hoping the others couldn't see that his eyes were screwed shut, suspecting that theirs might even be the same. Jesus wept! He had had such high hopes, such fantasies, and she was abso-fucking-lutely palsied!

And yet – when the scene, and the play, finished, and everyone raised their heads as if coming up for air, the luminous beauty of her face, eyes shining with a sweet, self-deprecating hope, snagged at his heart and overcame his judgement.

'So,' she said, and now that it no longer mattered her voice was soft and vibrant with a dozen complex emotions. 'How were we?'

Maurice decided to transfer her question from the particular to the general.

'Excellent,' he said. 'Well done everyone, I think we have a super cast and a sound safety net. Now there are just a few thoughts I want to send your way before we disperse...'

Half an hour later they left the hall on a wave of goodwill. Colin assured him that the production team was in place, and on the case. The good ship *Friday Fortnight* was launched, the sunny uplands of late summer stretched before them, the testing time of September was still far enough off to look forward to with a pleasure untarnished by the pressure of unlearned lines.

After his initial devastation, Maurice found that if anything he was even more smitten, and certainly that his emotions were now fully engaged. That Carolyn should have this Achilles heel, this perfectly blank spot, made her even more captivating in his eyes. After all, beauty stood alone, it was of itself and unassailable, one could only stand back and worship; but imperfection slipped under a person's radar and took possession of the heart.

Theirs were the last two cars in the car park. She gave him a little wave and called out softly, 'I'm afraid I was pretty hopeless.'

'Nonsense, it was all new to you.'

'No, no excuses, I'd read the play right through at home.'

'Reading aloud with other people is an entirely different exercise.' Why, he wondered, was he making excuses for her? Because, he answered himself, she was new to all this and anything else would have been churlish. Positive reinforcement at this stage was the best policy.

'You're so right!' She grimaced. 'Could do

better. Must try harder.'

He laughed. 'You'll be fine.'

'Au revoir, then. See you in September.'

'I look forward to it.'

On the way home he set about rationalizing. Plenty of people took time to get into character, and she'd been the most inexperienced one there. She was so obviously intelligent and intuitive, she'd catch on. And anyway, she was understudy, the likelihood was that she would never be on stage in public at all, at least in this production. He put on Barbara (his most secret vice) and clicked through the tracks to 'Evergreen'. For once, as the music swelled, he did not castigate himself for sentimentality.

A couple of days later, Diana called for the first time since their standoff. Both of them understood, though did not acknowledge, that the call was by way of an olive branch.

'How was the read-through?'

'Not bad. No absolute stinkers.' He told himself that he wasn't lying, because Carolyn was not in the cast. 'We'll get there.'

'I hope they appreciate you.'

'Oh they do, they do...' A reciprocal question seemed in order, so he asked: 'Everything all right on the Charlie front?'

'I made sure it was,' said Diana, with a sub-text of don't I always? 'He was mightily impressed with your loyalty, integrity, and all-round good-eggness.'

'I should think so.'

'As I still am, I must say.'

'I don't know why. I do have finer feelings.'

'Mm...' Maurice heard a cigarette being lit, and did the same. 'Maurice...'

'Diana.'

'I don't suppose there's a woman in all this, is there?'

'What on earth can you mean?'

'You heard me. You haven't conceived one of your monster pashes on the Greta Garbo of the Pear Tree Players?'

'Certainly not.'

'That sounds like a probably to me.'

'Take it how you want.'

'M-hmm.' Maurice could almost see the self-satisfied smile the other end, but was resolutely determined not to rise to the bait.

'So,' went on Diana after a pause. 'A quiet August for you.'

'I hope so.'

'Are you going away anywhere?'

'Jenny invited me down, but it's a crap time to go to Cornwall. I shall probably mooch around town – take in a few exhibitions, catch a film or two.'

'There are never any good films in August.'

'Plays, then. The trouble with plays is they always feel like homework.'

'Heaven forfend.'

'What about you?'

'I'm going walking in the Pelopponese.' Diana had a long history of spirited, challenging, single holidays.

'On your own?'

'No, with a small group. I'm looking forward to it.'

'Good luck to you.'

'Enjoy those exhibitions,' said Diana dryly.

August yawned by in its usual dreary way. It annoyed Maurice that everyone on TV and radio, and in the press, kept referring to this God-awful month as 'summer', as if it were the time they'd all been waiting for, when in reality all right-minded, grown-up people knew that August was the absolute arsehole of the season and it would be a colossal relief to reach September when the kids went back to school and normal service could be resumed.

The house near Daymer Bay to which his former (second) wife, Jenny, had invited him, presented no temptation. Cornwall was nice enough, but as far as Maurice was concerned it had always been Fulham-sur-Mer, full of prats in Guernseys, their Sloaney wives and 'young', which was how the wives referred to their petrifyingly confident, surfboarding children. Besides which Jenny herself was on the loose again, having recently separated from her second husband, and Maurice smelt an ulterior motive. Jenny, with two Dalmatians, a Porsche Boxster and a heavy shopping habit to support, was always hard up and he was a soft touch. Better to avoid temptation altogether.

So he mooched about. There were several very decent exhibitions and he enjoyed wandering round them alone, at his own pace, steaming past stuff that didn't interest him and sitting for half an hour if he so desired in front of a picture he liked. He had always been especially attracted by portraits, and now he found himself seeking out those supposed to be of famous beauties – actresses, hostesses, mistresses, anonymous girls with books and haughty chatelaines with fans – and subjecting them to rigorous scrutiny. None, in his opinion, could hold a candle to Carolyn Summerby. Even allowing for changing fashions in style, dress and physical attraction, and the fact that these women were inanimate images on canvas, she possessed a special luminosity, a delicately etched loveliness that outshone the competition. He wondered if anyone had ever painted her portrait. They must have done. The trouble was she was almost too beautiful. He could see it now, the chocolate-box perfection of the picture hanging over the mantelpiece or on the stairs, showing Carolyn in a long, shimmering full-skirted dress, hair and eyes gleaming in the light from a long window ... No one who had not seen her for themselves would be able to believe it was a true representation, and those who had would know all too well that it failed to do her justice.

He ached, he pined, he wallowed in the sort of luxurious, self-indulgent melancholy he hadn't experienced since his teenage years. Whenever he closed his eyes he could see her, she took up residence in his head and gently bore him company as he filled his desultory days. Was this love? Diana had been right about his 'monster pashes', he had always been prone to infatuations, they were as necessary to him as food and cigarettes and did wonders for his emotional circulation. Without exception they had evaporated once the princesse in question ceased to be lointaine. The exchange of bodily fluids signalled The End.

This time, he was sure, was qualitatively different. The difference was – It was – He shied away from framing the word but made himself do it: tenderness. Carolyn Summerby had uncovered a well of tenderness, of gentleness, of bloody altruism in Maurice that he had never known existed. Proof positive of this was the ease with which he had set aside her shortcomings (so devastating at the time) as an actress. The more time elapsed, the more distant she became, the less important that seemed, and the more he perceived it as heart-breaking, evidence of a poignant vulnerability that cried out for cherishing. He both did and did not want her to be obliged to tread the boards. Did, because of the opportunity it would present for greater contact and communication between them, for him to show a sympathetic understanding and sensitivity towards her; didn't, because he couldn't bear to think of her being disparaged and humiliated, talked about as a liability or even, God help us, a figure of fun. He couldn't really believe that would happen, they seemed a nice enough bunch of people, and hadn't Alice actually approached him with the request that he provide Carolyn with 'all the morale-boosting she could get'? But the capacity of amateur groups for bitchiness was legendary.

He worried about her. What was she up to now, during these dog-days? If his own former wives were anything to go by, divorced women no longer wasted a single calorie on self-pity or mourning what was gone – they got botoxed, blonde, and back in the marketplace before you could say GI Diet. But from what Alice had said it sounded as if Carolyn's case was slightly different – a shock, a genuine trauma, and fairly recent at that. Every time he thought about it he felt his jaws tighten and his fists clench. Bastard! How could he have done it? Even on the most brutally simplistic physical level it was hard to imagine another woman, even one young enough to be his daughter, more beautiful than Carolyn. Why, he himself had carried out an exhaustive survey of the most-admired women of the past five hundred years and it had failed to throw up even one!

One evening during the third week of August it occurred to him that he really should make the effort to inspect the Riverside Theatre where *Friday Fortnight* was to be put on. He couldn't imagine why he hadn't thought of this before, but now that he had he was enormously pleased with the idea. A visit to the Riverside was not just desirable but essential.

Excited and energized he set off next morning, booming up the motorway to the accompaniment of Bruce Springsteen, singing along and tapping his fingers on the steering wheel in a manner that positively screamed 'Twat!' when other drivers did it, but which was wonderfully mood-enhancing when one did it oneself. On a weekday morning it took him less than an hour to reach the town and, with the aid of the helpful brown signs, a further five minutes to locate the Riverside Theatre.

He had not emailed or telephoned in advance to advertise his arrival. He wanted to stroll around like a casual visitor, getting the feel of the place. Then, if he wanted to look backstage, or go on the stage itself, his credentials would provide the Open Sesame.

It was charming, as one might expect of a small, prosperous town within easy reach of London and in possession of a National Lottery grant. Every consideration had been given to providing a gemutlich experience – café-bar serving fusion food and light bites; terrace overlooking the river; foyer with gift and book shop; and a stylish, amphitheatre-style auditorium with no impeded views and ample leg room. The gents, when he sampled it on arrival, was perfectly adequate; the acid test would be the ladies, for an assessment of which he had for obvious reasons to rely on other people. As if in answer to his prayer he actually heard one middle-aged patron say to the other as they emerged: 'Well, that was a pleasant surprise.'

Another pleasant surprise was that the Pear Tree Players' production of *Friday Fortnight* featured in the 'Coming Soon' zone on the wall near the box office; there was a very decent poster and all the necessary information about dates, ticket availability and so on. He noted the optimistic strapline: 'Marlon Sibowitz's sparkling farce of morals, manners – and marriage!' Leaving aside that this description made the play sound almost contemporary, the adjective 'sparkling' was what really worried him. But perhaps it did no harm to tell people what to think. Politicians did it all the time. And the Players were not alone. If the publicity was to be believed, other forthcoming attractions included: '*A Laugh a Minute*: a feast of quick-fire gags from your favourite local stand-ups'; a touring production of *When We Are Married* with 'six of the country's best-loved actors' taking time out from Sunday night television; and

Ragweasel on the Road, described as 'the funniest, funkiest live children's show in years'. Maurice wondered what they put on for the dead ones.

Still, it all made the Players' self-promotion look perfectly respectable.

So far, so good.

Out on the terrace he ate a chicken and basil tortilla wrap washed down with a half of lager, and watched the swans gliding about on the river. Maybe it was the frowning black boss on their beaks, or the way they carried their heads, but it always seemed to him there was something innately stroppy about swans. Symbols of tranquillity and undying love they might be, but they were also as tense and edgy as football supporters stranded at an away game. Unresting, unhasting and silent as light ... Where did that come from? A dog on an extending lead got too close to the water and the cob steamed across with wings at the high port, scowling furiously. The dog was hauled back to a more circumspect distance but the swan continued to cruise parallel to the bank till the danger was past.

When Maurice had finished his lager he ordered an espresso and the bill, gulping down the one while paying the other. Down in the foyer he went to 'Riverside Reception and Information' and addressed himself to the young man behind the desk.

'Good afternoon. I'm Maurice Wolfe, I'm the director of a play that's being put on here in early October. *Friday Fortnight*.'

'Oh, right?' The youth spoke with one of those unnecessary upward inflections, the product of Australian soaps, that made the simplest remark sound like a question.

'I'd like if I may to have a look backstage, see what the stage is like, get the general picture. Would that be possible?'

'I don't know...' The youth looked doubtful. 'Do you have any ID?'

Telling himself that this was a perfectly proper request, Maurice fished out his card. As he did so the boy's face changed quite miraculously and Maurice was just congratulating himself on being better known, and among a different demographic, than he'd given himself credit for, when another voice said: 'No need to bother with that, Nathan, I can vouch for this gentleman.'

'Hallo, Mrs Summerby – I was just checking.'

'Of course!' She smiled at Nathan and Maurice, effortlessly disarming both of them. 'But this is Mr Wolfe, and he is a distinguished theatre director.'

'Sorry,' muttered Nathan, but Maurice's

attention was already elsewhere.

'Carolyn. What a nice surprise.' Nice? He who despised the word used it simply in order not to gush.

'I've been to the shop. It's rather good for birthday presents.' She touched his arm lightly to indicate that they should step back from the desk to make way for other people. When he did so he experienced a momentary flash of what it would be like to dance with her.

'...about you?' Her head was tilted slightly, he had the impression she might be repeating herself.

'I thought I'd come and take a look round. Get the feel of the theatre. I must say so far I'm impressed.'

'They got a grant.'

'I guessed as much. No, it's delightful.'

'Have you been backstage yet?'

'I was hoping to, but perhaps foolishly I didn't call in advance. That was what I was discussing with your young friend.'

'He's new, bless him, I know his mother, she's a client—'

'Client?'

'Oh...' She waved a hand. 'I sell hats. Anyway, the manager's a friend, he'll be pleased as punch you're here.' The other people had moved aside, and she leaned across and said: 'Nathan, I'll take Mr Wolfe to Mr Murray's office.'

'Okay.'

'I'll tell him you did all the right things.'

Nathan blushed. 'Yeah, thanks.'

'Do you know everybody, then?' asked Maurice, following her.

'Just about.' She laughed. 'Everybody's wife needs a pretty hat from time to time.'

He shook his head in admiration. She was wearing cream linen trousers, a white shirt, flat woven tan sandals. Her hair was a boyish crop, her face unmade-up.

Just before they reached the manager's door, Maurice stopped and asked, 'I don't suppose you'd like to look round with me? You seem to know everything that goes on around here, an insider's company might be very useful.'

'I'd so love to do that,' she said, with obvious sincerity, 'but I can't. I have to get back to the shop.'

'Of course – I was forgetting you're a businesswoman.'

'And a one-woman band at the moment. If I'm not there, hats don't shift. Anyway—' she tapped on the door – 'let me at least introduce you to Simon. You'll be in good hands.'

He heard, 'Come in!' and she opened the

door, extending her arm to usher him in.

'Simon, I've got a treat for you...'

On the drive home, the delicious, yearning melancholy that she engendered was tinged with the old excitement. It wasn't only the theatre he loved, it was theatres. The Riverside was charming, and he could already picture the auditorium packed with a loyal and enthusiastic audience, eagerly anticipating a sparkling farce presented by a local company ... Well, he'd make sure it was sparkling, dammit! That was what he was there for, to provide a high gloss, to turn a standard crowd-pleaser into something special; to help the Pear Tree Players (hadn't he said it himself?), and Carolyn in particular, be the best that they could be.

He arrived for the first rehearsal full of energy after the tedium of the past month, fired up and ready to go. It wasn't just the thought of the work, of doing what he did best, but of doing it in front of Carolyn, that gave the exhibitionist in him a distinct and delicious frisson. He longed, ached, to see her again, not just in his mind's eye. He wanted to strut his stuff, work with her, bathe in her appreciation and approval.

In short – it was terribly simple, and Maurice could no longer deny it – he wanted to be loved by her.

Love was always a long shot, he accepted that, but he could never have anticipated the swiftness with which the rest of his fantasy was fulfilled. When he arrived at the chapel hall, Colin met him at the door. The hall had been set out for blocking, with his table at the back, the chairs in a straight row in front, and a stage area marked out in white tape. The rest of the Pear Tree Players were standing in a ragged group inside this area, like sheep herded into a pen. All were wearing anxious expressions.

'Maurice,' said Colin, 'I hate to do this to you the moment you arrive, but I may as well cut to the chase.'

'Do, please.'

'I'm afraid Alice has had to drop out.'

'Never mind.'

Colin pulled his head back, chin in and eyebrows disappearing into his hairline. 'I beg your pardon?'

'These things happen. Better now than later.'

'I suppose.'

Maurice walked to the table and put his briefcase down next to the chair. From the corner of his eye he saw Carolyn come in –

283

sand-coloured cords, white shirt, loafers –
and stand at the end of the row of chairs.

'Evening!'

'Good evening...' they murmured watch-
fully.

'Hope you all had a good August. We'll
start in three.' He turned to Colin and spoke
in a low, concerned voice. 'Of course I'm
sorry about Alice, she was going to be good.
What happened?'

'She broke her leg on a hiking trip.'

'Damn shame. Give me her address, I'll
write.'

'I know she'd appreciate—'

Maurice raised his voice again. 'In the
meantime, we have an understudy, and we
shall use her, shan't we?' He turned to
Carolyn who, not having heard the first part
of the exchange, looked rather startled and
put a hand to her breast.

'Have I missed something?'

'Carolyn – you are our new Julia.'

'I am? I had no idea.' She glanced round at
the others with a self-deprecating little
laugh.

'None of us did, but short of rewriting the
entire role for a woman in a wheelchair with
her leg in plaster, neither of them helpful to
a femme fatale, that's what we shall do.'

'Poor Alice,' said Carolyn, cottoning on.

'How simply ghastly. And she was brilliant, too.'

'Then we owe it to her to be doubly brilliant,' said Maurice. He was on a roll, a high, he could not imagine that Charlie's luvvie revue could ever have been more intoxicating than this.

'Places for Act One, Scene One, please,' he said. 'The lounge of the Lugger Hotel. Mrs Flannery on stage, Miles and Fiona ready to enter stage right. Everyone got a pencil handy?'

Perhaps fortunately, they were all pretty terrible this evening, so Carolyn didn't stand out too much. The demands of moving about, reading while pretending not to, and jotting down notes, on top of the news about Alice, had a deleterious effect on morale and performance. All very understandable, as Maurice readily conceded. On the sidelines, Seamus had sat scowling jealously, marking the official pauses with sharp strokes of his pencil.

Maurice felt quite ashamed to be so happy.

By the time they'd blocked the first half everyone was tired, and he called it a day. Carolyn said, 'Sorry everyone,' and to Maurice, 'Couldn't Julia be tragically beautiful in a wheelchair?' which got a laugh and a small round of affectionate applause. She might be crap in the role, but people responded to her – how could they not? – and her stepping into the breach had a bonding effect.

While the chairs and table were being cleared, she came over to him.

'Joking apart, am I going to be able to do this? Seriously, Maurice?'

'Yes. Seriously Carolyn, you are.'

'You do understand that when I turned up late that night I was truthfully only looking to be a spear-carrier. I'm a complete novice. My last big role was the Virgin Mary at primary school and that was non-speaking. Thank God – no joke intended.'

'You're going to be fine,' he said. Greatly daring while trying to appear comforting, he placed a hand on her shoulder, which was slender and firm as a child's.

'Trust me.'

'Thank you.' She gave him one of her fine-tuned smiles, this time the wistful, rueful one. 'It looks as if I shall have to.'

The five weeks of intensive rehearsal were a heightened experience. Along with the usual highs and lows of production, the slowly mounting adrenalin and the occasional furious despair, was Maurice's feverish need to protect Carolyn, to tend and nurture her performance, even (he acknowledged it guiltily to himself) if that meant at the expense of others. By the week before production week the results could hardly be said to justify his efforts. Though conscientious and quick – she was only second to be word-perfect, never missed a cue or an entrance, and assimilated all her moves, including changes, instantly – but she was no actress. All the lively sensibility, the emotional sophistication, the warmth, humour and charm that came naturally to the real Carolyn drained away the moment she became Julia. She was wooden; her voice lacked resonance; she went through the motions but did not – he was beginning to think could not – inhabit the role.

Next week they would be locked in febrile, near-symbiotic interdependence with the production team with all the edgy power-play that inevitably involved. The get-in would be taking place over the weekend, the first run-through on stage would be on Monday night, followed by the technical and dress rehearsals ... Time was running out. Maurice could have wept to think that in eight days' time he would in all probability have failed her, and might never see her again...

He had had two successful meetings with the production team, the usual world-weary, dedicated bunch, convinced that everyone else was having fun poncing about while they did the real work, and individual members of the team had been along to watch rehearsals and make their lists and notes. He had tried to gauge their reaction, but they were mostly deadpan, very properly taking the view that the poncing bit was none of their business.

The single exception was the wardrobe mistress, Sally, a cheerful, approachable retired headteacher, whom he felt emboldened to ask outright, over interval tea: 'May I ask what you think of it?'

'Goodness, Maurice, you don't need my opinion.'

'I do. I'm interested. You've seen the Players before, presumably.'

'Most of them, you're right, there are a couple of new ones.'

'So?

'Fantastic, it's a real scream. You've worked wonders.'

'I've enabled them to work wonders.'

'However you want to put it. The pace, the timing, that's what I notice.'

'We've been working on that. Slow farce is

no farce.'

'Believe me it shows.'

They were standing by the portable rail of clothes that Sally had brought along; members of the cast had been trying on odd garments for fit and style during the course of the evening. Maurice brushed a hand along the clothes.

'What were you thinking of for Julia?'

'Well, I haven't got anything yet, but it should be full-on glamour, shouldn't it?'

Something in her tone prompted him to ask: 'How did you think she was doing? Carolyn was the understudy thrust somewhat unwillingly into the limelight. She's been a wonderful sport.'

'She's new, so she's one of the ones I don't know. She seems a bit – ill at ease.'

He nodded miserably. 'And that's not a very Julia-ish thing to be.'

'Not really. But she is absolutely stunning, and so elegant.'

'Maybe once we've got her into the fuck-off frock—' He checked himself. 'I do apologize.'

'I was a schoolmistress,' said Sally, 'not a nun. I've heard worse.'

'Then let's get her poured into something so sultry and sprayed on that the audience won't be able to think of anything else.'

'Leave it with me.'

Normally, he would have done – he was a firm believer in the absolute autonomy of different members of the team – but he wasn't sure that Sally, for all her excellent qualities, would know a truly fuck-off dress if it blacked her eye.

He had booked himself into a local hotel for the last ten days, a convenience factored into his generous fee. This meant that on the Friday of the get-in weekend he was able to invite everyone to have a drink with him at the eponymous Pear Tree, a pleasant coaching inn just up the road where, as Colin put it, 'the madness first started'. He was careful not to make a beeline for Carolyn, and in fact several of the others had gone, and she was slipping on her jacket, when he went over.

'Carolyn ... You're doing splendidly.'

'The best I can, anyway.'

'It's an absolute pleasure to have someone on stage who retains every single note.'

Her look of unalloyed pleasure made him feel like a heel and a hero at the same moment.

'Of course, you must look completely gorgeous. Which should be easy.'

'Oh!' She gave a little self-deprecating mou with a jerk of the head. 'That's too gallant of you.'

'But it's important to be comfortable. I was discussing this with Sally ... You could always wear something of your own.'

'You think?' She frowned, considering. 'I'm not sure Julia and I have the same style.'

You see? Maurice thought to himself over a nightcap in the hotel bar. She gets it, she understands Julia, she just can't do her.

Early the following morning Diana rang to wish him good luck. All was now completely restored between them.

'Just one last heave, then.'

'I'm looking forward to it.'

'And the cast?'

'They are, too. Once we get them booted and spurred they'll take off.'

'Yes,' agreed Diana. 'Clothes maketh the man, and the woman even more so.'

It was with these words ringing in his ears that he trawled the shops at lunchtime, in a break from the long attrition of set-building and lighting-installation. He had never chosen a dress for a woman, even Jenny, though he'd often footed the bill – the buying of women's clothes was women's work – but today he was on fire, moving from place to place like a tiger on the prowl for prey, restless, focused, driven.

He had set himself a tight budget – cheap things could look wonderfully glamorous on stage – and had not even completely ruled out that regular haunt of amateur wardrobe mistresses, the charity shop. However, he struck gold, literally, in a retail outlet touted by the Sunday papers as provider of economy bling to the nation's fashionistas. He had no idea what the fabric was, some sort of recycled plastic no doubt cobbled together in the sweat shops of Indonesia, but the frock was metallic, short, shiny, and hourglass-shaped even when on the hanger. And pleasingly cheap – when he walked out with it he had trousered change from twenty quid. At that price, even if Carolyn wouldn't wear it, and it only served to fire her imagination, it would have paid for itself.

As he headed back towards the Riverside, carrier bag swinging, he had no intention of going into any other shops; but as he passed Second Time Around a flash of colour as brilliant and arresting in those surroundings as a hibiscus in a privet hedge caught his eye, and he turned in.

The dress was hanging on a hook on the back wall. Also hanging on the wall were some pottery flying pigs, two Royal Wedding plates, a lacquered fan, a shell-framed mirror and a framed print of the The Haywain. But nothing could detract from the beauty of the dress. Maurice walked straight over to it and stood before it like a tourist gawping at a famous painting.

'Can I help you?'

He only half-turned to the assistant, unwilling to take his eyes off the dress.

'What size is this?'

'A ten, I think ... Let's see...' The woman couldn't reach, so Maurice took the hanger from the hook and passed it to her. When the scarlet satin brushed his arm it was thistledown soft.

'Hum...' The woman peered inside the bodice of the dress, front and back, and then inside the skirt. She called across to her colleague: 'Jan, do we know what size this dress is?'

'No, it's hand-made ... About a ten, I reckon.'

Maurice looked at the woman. 'Are you a ten?'

She shrieked with laugher. 'I wish!'

'I'll take it,' he said.

On Sunday evening the cast came to the Riverside for their first look at the set and an informal run-through on stage. The atmosphere was both flat and nervous, one

Maurice recognized and knew would pass. They were almost ready to be pushed off from the bank. Tonight he'd leave them alone; tomorrow he would give any last directions and be as positive as possible; on Tuesday they'd be subservient to the technical chaps. By dress rehearsal it would be out of his hands.

Before the run-through he waylaid first Sally and showed her his purchases, then Carolyn.

'I'm afraid the gold's hopeless,' said Sally. 'Too brash, and probably too short. But this...' she stroked the satin appreciatively. 'This is glorious.' She met his eye candidly. 'This could do it.'

Later Carolyn said: 'Oh? Whatever can it be?'

He took her over to the seat on the side aisle where he'd left the bag. The little theatre seemed cavernous with only them there, and a couple of lighting lads up on the gantry.

'I bought Julia a dress.'

'You did?'

'With Sally's approval. Or at least, Sally approved it.'

'How exciting!' She wasn't being in the least ironic. 'Let me see.'

Slowly, with an exquisite sense of display,

like a stripper peeling off stockings, he slipped the dress from its bag and held it up before her.

For several seconds there was complete silence. She was very pale, and her hands went slowly to cover her mouth. Her eyes shone, but they seemed cavernous. She seemed to be trembling.

At last, she whispered: 'Oh ... That?'

Maurice wasn't prepared. He had become used to her easy sophistication, her charm, her ability to finesse awkward moments and deflect potential embarrassment: this reaction was both disturbing and unreadable. To avoid it, he looked at the dress, swept his hand down its sensual length.

'You don't like it?'

She shook her head, her hands still over her mouth.

'You don't have to wear it,' he said. 'I picked it up in a secondhand shop.'

She blinked, and he saw that the shine in her eyes was due to tears, which now gleamed on her lashes and her cheek. This was so much the opposite of what he'd intended, he was devastated.

'Carolyn? I do apologize. I sense that I've put my foot in it.'

'No.' She was beginning to regain control. 'No, absolutely you haven't. I'm just a bit overwhelmed. Flattered that you could even imagine me in a dress like this.'

With a flash of inspiration, he said, 'The point is, I can imagine Julia in it.'

She folded her arms. After the first shock she hadn't looked at the dress and seemed determined not to touch it. 'Be honest. Do you want me to wear it?'

'Not necessarily, not if you don't want to.' He laid it back on the seat. 'I thought it might be a source of inspiration.'

'All right,' she said quietly, 'I see what you mean. You never know ... It might be.'

At the dress rehearsal night Maurice observed, not for the first time, how fine was the line between good acting and bad. It took very little, scarcely more than a thought, for woodenness to become intriguing understatement, for a banal delivery to transmute into something wondrously naturalistic. When an actor suddenly cottoned on, when they got it – that was pure magic. Alchemy.

There was very little about the mechanics of Carolyn's performance that had changed. She wore the clothes Sally had chosen, and yet from the moment of her entrance, and for the first time, she had become Julia. She carried with her Julia's special witty, wounded glamour, her air of emotional damage and her slightly ironic sophistication. All of this was so subtle that it hardly seemed 'acted' at all – it was simply there. Everyone felt it, and raised their game accordingly. When she rejected Miles' advances and turned him away, though she did it cruelly, for the first time it was clear that her pain was greater than his, though Dennis, too, had never been better. And when she made her little bitter-sweet speech to Fiona about being a good wife, you could have heard a pin drop.

Alice, now out of plaster but still on crutches, had come along to watch for the first time, and provide a fresh pair of eyes. On the final curtain she reached across and touched Maurice's arm.

'Congratulations,' she said. 'I'm jealous. I'd have played the damn thing as Long John Silver if I'd known.'

Maurice was terrified of breaking the spell. In his few words to them all on stage, he was careful to pick out no one for special mention.

'All I can say is that if the old adage is true we've set ourselves up for a terrible first night. Very well done everybody. You're on your own now. Break a leg.'

★   ★   ★

Gradually, over the next few days and nights, Maurice began the process of unravelling his connection with the Pear Tree Players. *Friday Fortnight* was a roaring success, sold out over all four performances and reviewed ecstatically in the local paper. Successive audiences adored it, howling with laughter, sighing empathetically and cheering the cast to the echo every night. Carolyn was faultless But next week he'd be gone, Diana had said that other work awaited his consideration and his cast would return, weary and slightly bedazzled, to pay much needed attention to their jobs and families. Carolyn to her hats, and her wide circle of admiring friends.

He gave the red dress to Sally, for the Players' wardrobe.

'Are you sure?'

'I've checked the diary – there's nothing I could wear it to.'

'Okay, okay,' she pulled a face. 'It's very kind of you.'

'And keep the gold one, too, splendid piece of cheap tat.'

'Thanks, it'll be great for panto.'

At the end of show party in the crush bar, Maurice had his hand wrung and his cheek kissed by everyone, sometimes more than once. They were all on a high, from which they were going to come crashing down, assisted by hangover hell, tomorrow. Maurice had learned to distance himself well in advance, so that by this time he was calm and ready to go, but they were clinging to the euphoria, and why not?

Only Carolyn didn't jump on him. They simply happened on one another, she in a corner waiting for someone to return with a drink, he in escape-mode. She was wearing a fawn silk shirtwaister and a big string of faux pearls, utterly perfect. How could she ever have worn the red dress?

His heart contracted in a sort of panic over what he was about to lose.

'I'm going to miss you all,' he said.

'And we shall miss you.' She took her glass from Dennis, who discreetly withdrew. 'I shall miss you.'

She hadn't needed to say that – his heart expanded again, swelled and leapt in his breast.

'I don't know if you're ever in London...?'

'As often as I want to be,' she said. 'It's not far, after all.' She seemed to be telling herself something, which he at once rushed to endorse:

'It's not! No distance at all.'

'I expect you're going to be frantically

busy. People to see, plays to put on.'

'All of that,' he agreed and added swiftly before he could change his mind: 'But I should very much like to see you.'

She said simply: 'I'd like that, too.'

'I'll be in touch then.'

'Please.'

He was buoyant with pleasure. She was the one person who hadn't kissed him, so he leaned forward and kissed her, and her skin was like satin, smooth and cool.

'Thank you, Carolyn,' he said. 'You were completely wonderful.'

'No,' she said softly, stepping back as others claimed him. 'Thank you.'